Scab

Scab

Robert Rayner

James Lorimer & Company Ltd., Publishers
Toronto

James Lorimer & Company Ltd. acknowledges the support of the Ontario Arts Council. We acknowledge the support of the Government of Canada through the Book Publishing Industry Development Program (BPIDP) for our publishing activities. We acknowledge the support of the Canada Council for the Arts for our publishing program. We acknowledge the assistance of the OMDC Book Fund, and initiative of Ontario Media Development Corporation.

Cover design: Meredith Bangay

Library and Archives Canada Cataloguing in Publication

Rayner, Robert
    Scab / Robert Rayner.

(SideStreets)
ISBN 978-1-55277-483-0 (bound).—ISBN 978-1-55277-482-3 (pbk.)

    I. Title. II. Series: SideStreets

PS8585.A974S33 2010   jC813'.6   C2009-906944-X

James Lorimer & Company Ltd.,
Publishers
317 Adelaide Street West
Suite 1002
Toronto, Ontario
M5V 1P9
www.lorimer.ca

Distributed in the U.S. by:

Orca Book Publishers
P.O. Box 468
Custer, WA USA
98240-0468

Printed and bound in Canada.

Manufactured by Webcom in Toronto, Ontario, Canada in February 2010.   Job # 366653

For Chooch and friends

Final Assignment

"A Letter to My Classmates"
For Mr. Kinney, English 1201
By Julian Faye

Dear Classmates,

At the end of our last year together, as we prepare for life beyond high school, I want to thank you for the way you welcomed me into your group twelve years ago, and for how you kept up your support and understanding nearly all the way through kindergarten, some of you even into Grade One.

I want to thank you for your gusts of laughter, year after year. You never tired of making fun of me. How stunned do you have to be to laugh at the same thing over and over again? Tell me, what was it exactly that made you all decide that it would be ME who would be tormented? Was it because I refused to play sports? (I could - still can - think of a hundred things more worth doing than flailing at a piece of rubber with a chunk of wood.)

Was it the way I talk? Was that the

first difference you thought worth mocking? I don't know what to say about it - the lisp you all so loved to imitate - except that I really can't help it. And, yes, you'll be pleased to know it distresses me, even whén I've had my whole life to get used to it. I'm not sure where it comes from; something to do with the cleft palate I was born with that took the doctors a long time to discover and fix. It's only a very slight impediment unless I get nervous. So of course you all made sure I was always nervous, never knowing when the cruel mimicry would begin.

You'll never know, because you could never be bothered to find out anything about me, that I feel the same scorn and contempt for you that you feel for me. You'll never know how much I despise your pulsating cars, with their radios blaring, your constant profanity (can't you finish a single sentence without saying fuck?), your guyness (the desperate need to conform to all its rules of bullying and bragging and putdown) and your chickness (your descent from the kindergarten innocence I still remember to the slutty clothes in music videos leaves me speechless).

Above all, I pity you your fear of anything and anyone that falls outside the orbit of what *you've* decided is normal. Congratulations on stumbling through this much of your narrow little world.

Thanks also for the nickname, Scab. I've become so used to it, that I now think of it as my name.

Limp on, losers.

Scab

SATURDAY, JUNE 13TH

11:35 A.M.
WATER STREET

The Crying Man is back on the street.

He stands in the doorway of an abandoned warehouse, weeping loudly. The sound rises above the hum and hiss of the traffic. The muscles of his face are knotted. His mouth gapes open, as if the sobs are being torn from him. He holds his hands to his face one minute, holds them in front of him the next, as if offering the weight of his suffering to the world. His cap is pulled so low it almost touches the upturned collar of his long khaki overcoat. His face is blotchy and red, stained with salty trails of dried tears. His chin is dark with two or three days' stubble. Wisps of grey hair straggle over each side of his face.

People on the street hurry past him. A few stop and stare. From where Scab stands, watching from an office doorway across the street, he can see some of them want to help. But the man's filth and smell hold them back. They look for somewhere to leave him money. Finding none, they too move on.

Scab's attention stays with the Crying Man. He has two cameras with him, the big Canon he uses for work and the little Olympus he always carries.

Holding the big camera ready, Scab gets the shot he's been waiting patiently for all morning: the man's face emerging from his hands, angled in just such a way that the overcast sky throws catch lights in his tears.

Perfect, Scab thinks. The photos are for a personal project he calls *Tears*.

He remembers the Crying Man on the streets when he was a kid. His mother looking steadfastly away, his father glaring at the unseemly display of emotion.

Scab lowers the camera for a minute.

When was the last time I cried?

He can't remember.

From his co-op work at the *Chronicle*, he's learned more about the Crying Man. He knows he was recently pegged for psychiatric observation after threatening a man with a knife. The Crying Man had sobbed as the judge told him he was tired of seeing him in court and made him swear — again — to be on his best behaviour. Then he was set free.

From the corner of the frame, Scab sees another familiar downtown character approaching. It's Road Safety Charlie. Scab watches as Charlie stops and cocks his head, listening to the Crying Man.

"Strong emotions can reduce your ability to think and react quickly, or make you more aggressive with other road users!" Charlie yells at him.

The Crying Man nods but continues weeping.

Charlie smiles and salutes as he passes, then continues down Water Street. Scab watches him go.

"Stay alert when driving at night, and whenever weather conditions reduce your visibility!" Charlie shouts over his shoulder.

Looking back, Scab sees that the Crying Man is no longer crying.

He lowers his camera. A couple approaches. The man is in tan pants and white shoes, the woman in pink tights and a long V-neck, a large silver bag slung over her shoulder. They carry unseasonable matching blue windbreakers.

Tourists.

Scab grips the camera more tightly — ready to record the scene. He could warn them, but that would spoil it.

The woman reaches into her bag. The Crying Man, still silent, seems to be staring past her. Scab follows his gaze and finds what he's looking at: the woman's big, silver hoop earrings. That glitter.

"You poor man," she says, nervously holding out a dollar.

Ignoring the money, the Crying Man suddenly

lunges at her. He grabs her earrings with both hands. She screams and falls back against her companion, who barks, "What the hell?" and pries the Crying Man's hands away.

The woman clutches her head tightly.

She's crying now.

The Crying Man is, too.

Across the street, Scab lifts his finger off the shutter button, but keeps the camera to his eye.

The tourists turn away from the Crying Man and cross the street towards where Scab skulks in the office doorway. As they approach, he fires off a few shots of the woman, mascara smudged, nose running, face streaked with snot and tears.

Scab hides the camera behind him as they pass. Then he checks the display. He smiles to himself, pleased with his work. *Time well wasted*, he thinks, and heads for work.

* * *

At the *Chronicle* by two o'clock, Scab heads over to check in with Foster Rent, Chief Photographer and his co-op supervisor. He's been promised one or two jobs for the afternoon.

He finds a note on Mr. Rent's desk.

> Scab, my man. Couple of things for you this fine Saturday afternoon.
> 2:00 P.M., North Side Food Bank, City Road. Minister for Social Welfare & MLA

*Joanne LeBlanc presenting cheque — a
grant from the province — for $5000.*

*3:00 P.M., Market Slip. Les Acrobats des
Etoiles, that circus troupe performing at
the Imperial Theatre, are doing some kind
of show on the boardwalk, then leading the
crowd (they hope) up King Street to the
theatre for the family matinee at 4:00.
It's just a promo stunt, but there might
be a picture or two in it.*

*Might catch you later.
F.R.*

Usual boring stuff, freeing up the staff
photographers for the important jobs. But Scab is
happy to get the work, for now, until he becomes
a fully fledged photojournalist somewhere —
anywhere.

He scrawls *Thanks* at the bottom of the note
and heads out.

. . . .

2:16 P.M.
NORTH SIDE FOOD BANK, CITY ROAD
The Honourable Joanne LeBlanc has coppery hair
teased into a fan around her head. She wears a
tight cashmere sweater tucked into expensive-
looking jeans.

"I want you to know, those of you who depend

on this food bank for your daily nourishment, that I know what it's like to be hungry," she says, leaning towards her audience at the North Side Food Bank.

Bullshit, Scab thinks. He's done his homework. He knows she's the daughter of a banker and the wife of a doctor. The only time she'd ever have been hungry was to starve herself skinny.

"I *share* your pain." The minister pauses to wipe a tear from the corner of her eye. Scab captures the act with his camera, and marvels at her ability to produce tears on demand.

"I *know* how important the work of this food bank and its volunteers is, and that is why your government is pleased to present this cheque . . ."

Scab feels a nudge at his side. The minister's aide — blue suit, red tie, hair slicked flat — is next to him.

"The minister would like some pictures showing her working among the homeless and needy," he whispers to Scab. He points to where the minister has now positioned herself between a woman and three men who have come in for food. Seeing Scab's camera, she blinks several times, producing fresh tears.

Scab walks out.

. . . .

3:15 P.M.
MARKET SLIP, DOWNTOWN
A ten-minute walk to Market Slip. The show has

already started when Scab arrives. A crowd of around a hundred watches as six men form a human pyramid. Another man is hoisted up, and does a headstand at the top. Then, a woman climbs up and stands on the feet of the man.

The crowd applauds.

Scab crouches low and shoots the stunt framed by the curve of the harbour bridge behind the acrobats.

The woman at the top suddenly loops to the ground in a series of hand-over-feet flips. The man below pushes himself into the air, somersaults once, and tucks and rolls as he lands. They join hands and bow as the remaining acrobats tumble down and line up behind them.

The audience applauds again and a flute begins to play. A piper in a tall hat and a pink-and-blue-checked suit appears. Someone in the crowd hands a young child to the acrobats in front. Carrying the child, they follow the piper, who leads them towards King Street.

Scab stands on one of the picnic tables that line the boardwalk to shoot them as they parade past. As he turns to go, he sees the Crying Man again, not crying, but staring at the gleaming water from the small rocky beach below the boardwalk. Scab watches him for a moment and shivers, though the air blowing in off the harbour isn't cold.

* * *

Back to the office on Crown Street. Scab could finish up on his computer at home, but he knows his parents are there. *Better the almost-quiet of the weekend newsroom than the silence of that house,* he thinks.

He works slowly. By the time he's finished downloading and working on his pictures — sharpening, adjusting contrast, and cropping them — and has chosen the best to leave for Mr. Rent, it's six o'clock.

As he waits for the elevator, Foster Rent arrives, talking on his cell. He holds up a finger. Scab waits.

"Bad accident on the highway. Truck and car," Mr. Rent says as he hangs up. "Want to come?"

. . . .

6:10 P.M.
SAINT JOHN THROUGHWAY
"Do you need to call your folks and tell them where you are?"

It's the only thing Mr. Rent says as he speeds out to the highway.

Scab shakes his head. He likes that Mr. Rent says very little. When he does speak, it usually requires only a short answer. The only time Mr. Rent says more is when he is at his apartment, drink in hand.

For the past two years Scab has been visiting Mr. Rent's apartment. The photographer took him under his wing when he was just a middle-school kid sending pictures to the *Chronicle* for the "News from the Schools" page. Mr. Rent had visited Scab's parents, offering to give him photography lessons. Since then Scab has learned something about Mr. Rent's past as a photo-journalist — how he made a name for himself for his photos of the Vietnam war, and how he'd won awards for his coverage of conflict all over the world, before giving up his globetrotting to settle in Saint John. He'd even loaned Scab the big Canon, saying, "No need to mention it to anyone. It's just an old one I found lying around the office."

As the flashing lights of emergency vehicles come into view, Mr. Rent says, "This may not be pretty. There's a kid involved. You'll be okay?"

Scab nods.

Mr. Rent drives the car onto the median and stops. He and Scab grab their cameras and walk past the stalled traffic towards the lights. When they are close, a police officer blocks their way and says, "You can't —"

"Hi, John."

The cop peers at them. "Oh, Mr. Rent."

"Bad, is it?"

"It's real bad. The woman pulled out in front of the truck. I don't think she even looked. The trucker didn't have a chance to stop. There's a kid. Looks like he's . . ." The cop breaks off, glancing uncertainly at Scab.

Mr. Rent says, "Say hello to Julian Faye. He's with me at the *Chronicle*."

The cop nods at Scab and stands back to let them pass.

Scab follows Mr. Rent. They walk alongside the truck, which is stopped in the right lane. Scab can't see any sign of an accident. It's as if the truck, and all the traffic around it, had simply stopped.

Just then, Mr. Rent takes one of his cameras from his shoulder, and moves quickly to the front of the truck. He drops to his knees and starts to photograph. "Oh Jesus," he mutters.

All Scab can see is the truck, and a crowd of police and firemen milling around. He's still wondering what Mr. Rent is shooting, when he sees the car. It's wedged, almost flattened, under the truck. Scab kneels beside Mr. Rent to take a few of his own shots, careful to keep out of his boss's way.

"Here's the kid," Scab hears someone say. At the same time he notices two pairs of feet on the other side of the truck.

Scab walks around the back of the truck, coming up alongside the cab. A fireman and a paramedic are standing there, looking up at the driver's window, talking softly. Scab inches forward.

The truck driver.

He's still in his seat, staring. His hands are frozen on the steering wheel. Scab hears one of the rescuers call out urgently, "Take the kid. We've got to get the woman out."

The paramedic and the cop hurry away, leaving the driver in the cab. As Scab watches, the door opens slowly and he climbs out. As if in a trance, the trucker drifts in behind the crowd of rescuers.

Scab follows.

A bundle is passed back through the rescuers, who are now trying to free the trapped woman. Someone is saying, "Gently. Easy does it . . ."

A rescuer at the back of the crowd receives the bundle and, without looking, hands it behind him, where the truck driver takes it in his arms.

Scab raises his camera in time to capture the event. Cradling the bundle, the driver turns back towards his truck. He squats to sit on the metal step. Scab grabs a few shots of him gazing down at the child in his arms before paramedics rush up, grab the child, and lead the driver to an ambulance.

Scab stands motionless, still seeing the blank expression on the driver's face. *What's it like, to be beyond any expression of guilt, or remorse, or grief?* Scab searches his emotions for how he himself feels. *Shouldn't I feel something?*

Mr. Rent calls from the rear of the truck, "I'm done. How about you?"

Scab nods. As they walk back to the car, Mr. Rent asks, "What have you got?"

He takes Scab's camera and scrolls through shots of rescuers working to free the driver and the child from the wreckage. He slows when he reaches the pictures of the cop and paramedic trying to talk the trucker out of his cab, and stops at the first shot of the truck driver cradling the child's body.

"Jesus, Scab. How did you get this picture?"

Scab shrugs. "Jusht lucky, I guessh."

The lisp.

"Lucky, my arse. How did you know to go around the other side of the truck?"

Scab shrugs again.

Mr. Rent stares at Scab's shots of the driver looking down at the child he has just killed, his face frozen.

"He'll be carrying that child for the rest of his life," Mr. Rent mutters, and shakes his head. "We can't use these pics in the paper, of course. Bad taste and all that. But . . . Christ, Scab. When you've made a name for yourself and can take the heat for taking pictures like this, show them then." He hands the camera back. "Scab, my man, you're older than your years. It's one thing for a hardened old fart like me to keep shooting when he comes on a scene like this, but for a seventeen-year-old . . . I don't know . . . You're either a callous bastard, or some kind of one-in-a-million artist." He looks at Scab, suddenly grinning. "Which one?"

As Scab opens his mouth to reply, a fire truck pulls out, siren wailing.

Mr. Rent says, "Our lucky night. Let's see what's going on."

* * *

From the overpass, Scab is the first to see the smoke and flashing lights below. "There!" he says.

"It's the old City Hotel. We'll take the back way in. We won't get near it from the front. Hold tight."

Mr. Rent pulls the wheel hard to the right and they just make it onto the exit ramp they were passing. He speeds through a network of narrow streets lined with houses and stops the car on a patch of wasteland two blocks behind the City Hotel.

. . . .

7:35 P.M.
CITY ROAD

"Sit this one out if you like," Mr. Rent says, getting out of the car.

Scab shakes his head.

They make their way across the wasteland until the back of the hotel looms before them. The lights of the rescue vehicles reflect on the smoke billowing above the roof. There are no flames. As they round the building, Scab sees the police have roped off the area in front of the hotel. A crowd of spectators watches from behind the barrier. Some clutch clothes and bags. Scab realizes they are hotel guests who have fled the fire.

Mr. Rent says, "Usual drill. Keep clear of the

rescue guys. Their job's more important than ours," and moves cautiously towards the barrier to shoot the front of the hotel. Two police gesture at him to get behind it, but he holds up his camera and they nod.

Scab starts to follow but stops in the shadows. Alongside the hotel is a van. 'Les Acrobats des Etoiles' is written on its side.

He looks along the front of the hotel. Mr. Rent has found a spot where he can include rescue vehicles in his shots, as well as zoom in on firefighters. Scab can see them as though through Mr. Rent's lens — silhouetted against the smoke, the effect making it appear as if they are about to be engulfed by it.

Scab looks around for a different shot. He lifts the camera and scans the hotel guests huddled at the front of the watching crowd. Among them he recognizes the acrobats he saw earlier. He photographs their faces, the lights of the rescue vehicles lighting them up in garish red and gold.

He tries to read their expressions, but can't. They'd just had to flee from a fire. What would he feel in their situation?

One of the acrobats pushes through the crowd. "Where's Emma?" he yells at the woman acrobat Scab saw perform earlier that day.

"I thought you had her," the woman replies.

"I thought *you* had her," the man shouts.

The man ducks under the barrier, ignoring the

police who order him to stop, and runs towards the awning that leads to the hotel entrance. Two fire-fighters grab at him but he glides nimbly between them and runs inside.

From the nearest fire vehicle, suited-up firefighters immediately appear. They are masked and carry oxygen tanks on their backs.

They look like spacemen, Scab thinks as he photographs them plodding towards the hotel. Eye to the viewfinder, he sees a sudden bright glare through the windows on either side of the hotel entrance. Seconds later there's a shattering of glass, and a cascade of flames pours out.

Like an upside-down waterfall . . . a firefall, he thinks. His camera shutter opens and closes to catch the colour of the flames against the darkness of the building and the sparkle of glass shards.

He sees the reflection of the flames in the smoke above.

The balance of form and colour.

The contrasting tilt of the crowd leaning towards the fire and the firefighter-spacemen lurching backwards as the fire erupts.

Scab feels a thrill. That moment now belongs to him.

As the firefighters gather themselves and plod forward again, a supervisor near him shouts, "Wait!"

The fire at the centre of the building is creeping outwards towards each end.

Scab shifts his camera slightly, spotting movement in a second-floor window. He zooms in and sees the acrobat, now clutching the child he and the woman had held earlier that day in the parade. Scab takes two shots before lowering his camera a little to look around for rescuers.

It's their job to spot trapped people, isn't it? How come they're not seeing this? he wonders.

He looks back up at the window with his naked eye. The man has tucked the child under his arm and is leaning out against the window frame. He shouts something Scab can't hear over the crackle and hiss of flame and the commotion of the crowd.

Scab raises the camera back to his eye and zooms in tightly on the man, photographing him as he moves to hold the child out the window. Scab thrills again at the picture he's getting: the man's anguished expression, the glow of the flames lighting one side of his face, the other side shadowed in darkness, the child's chubby arms waving, its mouth and eyes wide open, in terror . . . or excitement.

Rescuers are going to notice any second now, Scab thinks, mentally refusing to lower his camera. *Then the scene will be over. It's too good not to keep shooting.*

He's closer to the window than anyone, but surely someone else will see or hear. The man is yelling again. Through the lens of the camera, the acrobat seems to make eye contact with Scab.

Scab thinks he lip-reads the word, "Catch . . ."

Startled at what is about to happen, Scab decides that it is time to call for help. But in that instant, the man moves slightly. Now he's perfectly framed by the window.

Just one more . . .

The man climbs onto the sill and balances there. Still holding the child, and with the fire drawing closer and roaring louder, he launches himself forward. As he falls, his loose-fitting clothing billows out like wings so that he seems like that mystical bird — a phoenix — flying out from the flames. Scab hears the gasp from the crowd, and knows they've noticed now. He feels the pounding of boots on cement as firefighters run over to where Scab stands.

Scab holds his finger down on the shutter, recording the acrobat's flight to the ground.

As the man lands, he tucks and rolls, still holding the child tightly against his chest. Fire leaps from the window where he stood seconds before. The child is safe in his arms. The crowd, and some of the rescuers, applaud. The man bows, as if this were all part of a performance by Les Acrobats des Etoiles. The mother rushes from the crowd, seizes the girl and, kneeling, cradles her. The father sinks down beside the woman, while the firefighters surround the reunited family. Scab stops photographing when the fire official, moving towards the group, sees him and gestures for him to put the camera down.

Scab lowers his camera, waits until the official turns away, and then takes a few more shots.

Mr. Rent calls, "Scab, my man, let's go!"

As they set off, the man from the window looks up at them and calls, "I was shouting, 'Catch the kid.'"

Scab keeps walking.

Mr. Rent says, "What's he saying?"

Scab shrugs. "Dunno."

The father shouts louder, "You — you with the camera — didn't you hear me? I was shouting 'Catch the kid.'"

Mr. Rent glances at Scab.

Scab keeps walking.

. . . .

11:00 P.M.
FARM CRESCENT

Back home, his mother appears as soon as Scab opens the door.

"Did you have a nice time, dear?"

What's it to you? he thinks.

"I'm busy, Ma," he says instead.

Scab goes upstairs to his room. He takes the press badge from around his neck and throws it on the bed. The photo lands face up. Long thin face, pale complexion, limp black hair that always seems greasy no matter how often he washes it. *Like a cartoon undertaker,* he thinks.

He turns the photo over so he doesn't have to look at himself.

28

Sitting down at his desk, Scab connects the camera to the computer. While he waits for the pictures to download, he glances around at the prints — his prints — pinned up on the walls. Shoppers elbowing at a crowded stall in the city market, sunburned holidaymakers eating at a hot-dog stand on a city beach, teens shrieking on a carnival ride at night, a three-legged dog cowering in a shop doorway. He's hopeful that one of the evening's shots will be good enough to join the images hanging there.

A picture of the father at the window, holding the child out, appears on the computer screen. The man's mouth is open, calling. What did the father claim he was shouting? *Oh yeah, "Catch the kid."*

Scab wonders, briefly — if he had reacted, could he have caught the child?

Probably not.

But the firefighters could have managed it — they had special equipment, maybe even a net or something, for catching people jumping from windows.

Except they would have been too late. The fire was spreading too fast.

So there was nothing anybody could have done to help, he decides. All he could do was record the moment, which he had done.

He goes downstairs to phone Mr. Rent.

"What?" the familiar voice says. Scab grins at how Mr. Rent answers the phone.

"I got shome . . . shome . . ." The sibilants are whistling outrageously.

Scab stops. Talking to Mr. Rent doesn't usually bother him. He must be more wound up than he thought.

Mr. Rent says, "Easy."

He tries again. "I got shome . . . shome good shtuff."

I sound like a retard, Scab thinks. Was he just tired? Or was it the excitement of the accident and the fire? Something about the driver and the baby? The father and child at the window?

"Better than my stuff?" Mr. Rent asks.

"Courshe not."

"But good enough to interrupt me when I'm prepping my pics — right?"

Scab doesn't answer.

"I'm kidding."

"I know."

He doesn't know. He's never sure with Mr. Rent. It forces him to evaluate every picture before presenting it to him. Mr. Rent's criticism could be brutal.

"Anything good enough for Monday's paper?"

"Think sho."

"Okay. Send me two or three of the best shots."

Scab runs up to his room to e-mail the pictures, then goes back down in search of something to eat.

His mother is in the kitchen in her dressing gown. Her hair looks like a white-and-grey cumulus cloud has settled on her head. Her glasses perch halfway down her nose. Through the doorway, Scab glimpses his father seated in his armchair, watching the news. He hears a report on bickering politicians give way to an item on the hotel fire. Scab moves a little into the room so he can see the TV screen. A reporter is describing the spectacular rescue of the child, and the camera sweeps across the front of the hotel. Scab can clearly see himself now, photographing from the shadows, illuminated by the flames. He waits for a comment from his father. It doesn't come. The news moves on to another story.

The phone on the wall behind him rings.

Mrs. Faye looks at Scab. "Why don't you answer it?"

Scab shrugs. He hates answering the phone.

Mrs. Faye picks it up. She purses her lips and passes the phone to him.

Mr. Rent says, "Nice work," and hangs up.

"I wish you'd answer the phone, Julian," Mrs. Faye grumbles. "Or get yourself a cell phone."

"Can't afford it, not with having to save up for college. Why don't you get me one?"

"You can talk to your father about that."

"Like he'll even listen." He looks at his father, still watching the news.

Mrs. Faye, following his glance, says, "I'm making him some tea. Would you like a cup? I'll bring it in for you. You could watch the news together."

Scab shakes his head. He takes a container of yogurt from the refrigerator.

"How about something more to eat than just a yogurt?"

"No."

"I could make you a toasted cheese sandwich."

"Nah."

"Or a peanut butter and jam sandwich. I always used to make you a peanut butter and jam sandwich when you got home from school."

You were never here when I got home from school.

"Remember how much you used to like them?"

I'd sooner eat dog shit than a peanut butter and jam sandwich.

"This'll do. Thanks."

"How about a nice glass of milk, with some cookies?"

Why don't you warm the milk, while you're at it, and put it in a bottle, and stick a nipple on the end? Do you think that'll make up for farming me out every day when I was a kid, so you could haul yourself up the corporate ladder?

He shakes his head.

"Have you been out with your friends?

What friends?

"I told you this morning — I was taking pictures."

"You might have been photographing with friends. Like in a club. You could join a photo club."

32

And hang around with a bunch of pretentious wannabes.

"How many times do I have to tell you? I don't want anyone with me when I'm taking pictures."

"You don't have to growl at me like that, Julian, just for asking. Just for suggesting."

"Sorry."

"Anyway, you don't seem to mind Mr. Rent."

"Mr. Rent's different."

"I'll say he's different."

"What's that supposed to mean?"

"Him a grown man, hanging around with a boy."

"We don't hang around. We take pictures. He shows me stuff. He asked you, and you said it was okay — remember?"

"It just seems funny, a grown man giving up his time for a teenager. I hope he doesn't tire you out, giving you all this photo work to do, on top of your studying."

"What studying? School's as good as finished. It wouldn't matter if I didn't go anymore."

"But you should spend the last few weeks of term with your classmates."

That'd be the classmates who've been making my life a misery for the last twelve years? Sure, why not.

"School friendships are so special."

I hope I never see any of them again.

"You'll at least go to graduation, won't you? It'll make your dad and me so proud, to see you walk across the stage and get your diploma."

Scab looks into the living room at his father again. "Don't think so."

"Your dad might have something to say about that."

Like I'll be listening.

SUNDAY, JUNE 14TH

5:35 P.M.
FARM CRESCENT

Scab stands at the mirror in his room, willing himself to cry.

He tries thinking of the starving children in Kenya he's seen on TV.

No effect.

He pictures the homeless people he sees huddled every night in the entrance to the liquor store near his home.

Nothing.

He thinks of pleading panhandlers, like the Crying Man, that he sees on the streets of the city.

Still nothing.

He thinks of his grandmother, who died a few

months ago, and pictures himself as a little kid, sitting on her lap as she reads to him. He'd liked that.

But even then, no tears come.

He finds some mournful music on his computer and invents an accompanying movie scene, the end of an affair, the girl walking quickly away, the boy watching her go, then turning up his coat collar — it's raining, of course — and thrusting his hands in his pockets, certain that he will never love again.

Pathetic idiot.

He's been looking at his *Tears* collection, and wants to include his own crying in it. His tripod-mounted camera is focused on his image in the mirror, and the cable release is ready in his hand, but he can't cry.

He wonders if he can inflict enough pain on himself to produce tears. He thinks of a picture he has captured of a child in a park, whom he saw running, and falling, and sliding in gravel, lacerating hands and knees. He'd taken three frames before the mother scooped up the child. He takes scissors from his desk and, watching himself in the mirror, stabs the back of his hand.

It hurts like hell — but no tears come.

He stabs himself again, this time in the fleshy part of his bare arm.

He sees himself wince, but still he can't seem to cry.

Is there something wrong with me?

Looking at himself steadily in the mirror, he places the sharp tip of one blade against the soft tissue of his face just below the eye and carefully breaks the skin.

No tears, but blood this time. It oozes and pools for a moment at the lip of the wound before starting to roll slowly down his cheek, a bloody tear.

Quickly, he cuts himself under the other eye and, as a second bloody tear rolls down his face, releases the shutter.

His mother calls out, "Julian, supper."

He stops the bleeding and cleans his face.

* * *

Scab and his parents eat in silence. Mr. Faye watches a football game through the open door of the living room. As soon as he finishes, he returns to his chair in front of the TV.

Scab finishes next, and takes his dishes to the sink. Mrs. Faye follows, carrying her own plate, and her husband's. Before Scab can make for his room she says, "You'll be going to school in the morning, won't you?"

Will I?

"You should go — for your father's sake. He wants to see you graduate."

"I'll graduate. My marks are okay and I'm already accepted for photojournalism at Loyalist College."

"I mean he wants to see you at graduation, so he can boast about you at work, and tell his friends about his boy, who's soon going to be at work with him. You know he's been promised a summer job for you, as well as something permanent in the fall."

"I've told you a hundred times — I'm not working at the mill. I told him, too. That's why he hasn't spoken to me for two weeks."

"What's wrong with working at the mill?"

"Nothing. It's just not what I want to do."

"Because that Mr. Rent has filled your head with unrealistic dreams about being a photographer, like him. The mill was good enough for your father, and it's good enough for you, too."

I'm nothing like him.

"Mr. Rent got you a place at college, but he's not paying your tuition, is he? You'll expect us to pay."

"Mr. Rent didn't get me a place. All he did was recommend me. And I told you — Loyalist College is giving me a full scholarship."

"What about accommodation and meals and so on?"

"There's an allowance for that, and I'll earn a bit at the *Chronicle* in the summer."

"Not enough to cover everything. Your father's going to charge you rent if you don't take that summer job at the mill, so that'll take most of what you earn. Why don't you do what he wants?"

Scab shrugs and turns to leave.

Mrs. Faye calls after him, "He wants what's best for you." Something in her voice makes Scab pause in the doorway and look back. Her eyes are shiny. He fingers the little camera in his pocket.

"You don't care about your father and me. All you care about is yourself." She covers her face with her hands and sobs.

He says gently, "Ma . . ."

She lowers her hands to look at him and he shoots two quick frames before she gasps, "How could you? What's *wrong* with you, Julian?"

From the desk of Dr. W.F.S. Furlong Ph.D. M.A. B.A.

CONFIDENTIAL

Subject: Julian Faye   **Age: 17 years**

Subject was referred after exhibiting anti-social behaviour (withdrawal, hostility, passive-aggression) towards both peers and authority figures, and having difficulty in forming and maintaining relationships over the course of his school career.

Throughout testing and interviews, subject was non-compliant, veering between hostility and withdrawal into silence.

Tests and observation suggest subject suffers from borderline Schizoid Personality Disorder (SPD), a condition characterized by excessive detachment from social relationships, a restricted range of expression of emotions in interpersonal settings, a dislike of talk, and difficulty responding appropriately to important life events. Because of their lack of social skills, individuals with this disorder have few friendships. The disorder is usually first apparent in childhood with solitariness, poor peer relationships, and underachievement in school, which may attract teasing from peers.

Dr. W.F.S. Furlong Ph.D. M.A. B.A.

MONDAY, JUNE 15TH

9:50 A.M.
HARBOURSIDE HIGH SCHOOL

Scab silently curses himself for not getting out of the classroom faster. And for giving in to his mother's pleas the night before, and again in the morning, to go to school.

All the other students spill out into the hallway at the end of first period. Mr. Kinney, the small, round-shouldered English teacher, gestures for Scab to stay.

"I saw your pictures of the hotel fire in the paper this morning. They were very good."

So you're a photo critic in your spare time.

Mr. Kinney perches on the desk at the front of the room. Scab stays where he is, just inside the door.

"You obviously have an eye for a photograph."

Now I'm supposed to fall all over myself thanking you for trying to say something nice?

Mr. Kinney looks at Scab as if he expects him to respond.

Scab looks at the floor.

"So . . . ah . . . well done!"

More silence from Scab.

"Well . . . ah . . . let's get down to business." Mr. Kinney produces Scab's assignment. "I'm sorry, but I can't accept this."

"Why not?"

"It's inappropriate. It's bleak and unpleasant and offensive."

Scab shrugs. "You shaid to write a letter to our clashmates shaying how we felt about parting after going through shchool together."

"I didn't mean you to attack and insult your classmates."

What did you expect? They've been attacking and insulting me for twelve years.

"I'd like you to do the assignment again. I think you'll feel better if you give it a more positive tone."

It'll make you feel better, you mean. You won't feel so guilty about what I've had to put up with all through school.

"If you refuse, I'm afraid I'll have to give you a fail. It will make no difference to your marks at this point. But, Julian, it's not a good way to end your high-school career."

"Shuit yourshelf."

Mr. Kinney stands abruptly. "Is that all you've got to say?"

Scab slips his hand into his pocket, reaching for the little camera. It's an involuntary action. He's raising it to his eye, to put it between himself and Mr. Kinney, when the teacher snaps, "Put that thing away."

"It'sh called a camera."

"I know what it's called, and you're not taking my picture with it."

Scab becomes aware that he is blinking rapidly. "I was jusht going to look through it."

Mr. Kinney sighs. "I'm sorry. I didn't mean to raise my voice. But it's really better that you don't do that. People want to see your face, not a camera pointed at them."

Scab slowly returns the camera to his pocket.

Mr. Kinney says, "You know your mother asked me to talk to you?"

Scab knows. His mother told him as he was leaving that morning that she'd asked "that nice Mr. Kinney" to speak to him about being a loner. It was her latest effort — and would soon be her last, Scab remembers with relief — to integrate him into high-school life. *And, no doubt, make up for dumping me when I was a kid,* he thought. The memory of a nanny who was all over him if his mother was there, and ignored him as soon as she left, flooded back to him. Eventually it got so that solitariness became a habit he couldn't break.

When his mother had been forced to retire from her position as Project Manager with the power company a year ago, she'd suddenly wanted to make up for years of ignoring him. But he wasn't going to let himself become her latest — guilt-driven — project.

Scab tunes back in to Mr. Kinney. "Your mother worries about your not having any friends."

Scab stays silent.

The teacher leans forward, clasping his hands in front of him. "You're not helping yourself with this attitude, you know."

"What attitude?"

"The attitude that makes people . . . dislike you."

Like I care.

"I know it's difficult for you, but you could make more of an effort to be accepted by your peers, instead of deliberately setting yourself apart. You think you can do without friends, but you'll find you're wrong."

The bell rings again to signal the start of second period.

"Are we done?" Scab asks.

Mr. Kinney sighs again, and nods.

Scab slips out of the classroom.

* * *

Midday. The hallway, crowded with students,

crackles with sexual tension and looming threat. Scab eases himself through the crush, keeping his head down. He finds his way blocked by a group of his classmates. A tall, soft-featured boy with a mop of fine blonde hair leans against his locker. Two girls are pressing themselves up against him.

"Where do you think you're going, *Julie Scab?*" the boy asks.

Go fuck yourself, Brett Hanley, Scab thinks as he tries to pass.

He brings the camera to his eye.

The boy instantly falls back, hands in his pockets, slouching. "Go on, then. Take my picture."

The girls drape themselves on each of his shoulders. Scab presses the shutter and holds the monitor toward the group.

Brett preens. "Hey, cool. You'll do a print of that for me — right?"

Scab nods. School has always been like this, one confrontation after another to be avoided. Keeping his head down, Scab picks his way through the crowd, deleting the picture as he goes.

FRIDAY, JUNE 19TH

6:30 PM.
FARM CRESCENT

"Are you going out tonight, dear?" Scab's mother asks after supper on Friday.

You think I'm going to spend the evening watching TV with you and Pa?

Scab nods.

"With friends from school?"

You know I don't have any friends from school.

"I'm taking pictures of a group from the Baptist university. For my *Night in the City* project."

The project is part of his co-op work. Mr. Rent has arranged to run it in the *Chronicle*.

"Oh. *Oh!* That'll be nice. They'll be nice young

people to be friends with." She looks at Scab's father. "Won't they, Gorman?"

Mr. Faye grunts without looking up from the newspaper that's spread open beside his empty plate. Scab's father has wide, straight shoulders, and his neck is so short his bald head seems planted in them. His eyebrows are thick and grey, and his nose is florid and slightly bent, giving his face a misleadingly jolly appearance.

He looks like the perfect grandfather.

Except he's Scab's dad.

And he doesn't behave like a grandfather. As far as Scab knows, grandfathers lavish time and attention on their grandchildren. All Scab feels from his father is hostility and resentment.

Scab collects his cameras from his room.

His mother hovers at the foot of the stairs. "What time will you be home?"

Can't I leave the house without this charade every time?

"Don't know."

"I'll wait up for you, shall I?"

"Don't bother. I'll be late."

"I will, anyway. Have a nice time, dear. Have fun with your new friends."

She moves towards him. Scab's afraid she's going to hug him.

He steps quickly past her and out the door. At the end of the driveway he looks back. She's in the doorway, waving. He knows she's as friendless as he is, although it's not his fault she has nothing to

47

do now that she's not working. She fusses all day over his father and him. And gets nothing back for her efforts.

Scab nods and sets off through Farm Crescent, past houses just like his own. They are evenly spaced, with lawns in front and driveways leading to double garages. He often notes with satisfaction that the backyards, at least, are different. Some sport flower beds and lawns and gravel paths, others have plots of soil ready for vegetable planting, or worn-out kitchen appliances rusting among unkempt grass.

He catches the downtown bus at the foot of his street. As he watches the subdivisions go by, he tries to decide how he feels about his hometown. He has no great urge to leave this place, yet none to stay either.

It's another way he feels separate from his peers. Some of them can't wait to escape the boredom of Saint John, while others talk about their hometown with affection, already looking forward to the school reunion they'll attend after their first year at the Saint John campus of the University of New Brunswick. Scab looks at both attitudes with equal contempt, but he wonders whether there's something wrong with him.

. . . .

8:05 P.M.
ATLANTIC BAPTIST UNIVERSITY
The Baptist university is a ten-minute walk from

the downtown terminal. It's housed in a brick
building that was formerly the Saint John Mental
Health Institute. Most people still call the
property, with its high iron fences, "Asylum
Park." Scab tramps through the park to the main
entrance and pulls open the heavy wooden door.
His footsteps are loud on the stone floor of the
entry hall. He crosses to a handwritten sign taped
to the wall.

Outreach Endeavour
2nd floor, Room 208
8:00 P.M.

There's no one around, but he can hear voices
as he makes his way up the curving staircase to
room 208.

The door to the room stands ajar. From inside,
he hears a man speaking loudly. "I'm afraid we
may have to curtail our mission with the city's
homeless because the university, as one of its cost-
cutting measures, is dropping our funding. This
means we'll have to rely solely on donations and
our own fundraising. The van, I fear, will be the
first thing to go."

Scab hears a soft murmuring from the room. He
waits out of sight as the voice continues. "So,
assuming we can still raise enough money to pay
for blankets and food, we'll be going on foot in
the future. Now — to the present. Our target this
evening is the area around the intersection of City

Road and Waterloo Street. And we have a guest coming with us tonight, a Mr. Julian Faye, a young photographer who ... ."

In the hall, Scab recoils from the sound of his own name. Afraid that whatever the man says next will draw even more attention to him, he steps into the half-open doorway and taps on the door.

The speaker, a thick-shouldered and jowly man with long hair pulled back in a ponytail, strides to meet him.

"A young photographer . . . who, I'm guessing, is you!" He wears a broad smile and holds out his hand in welcome.

"I'm Greg Fleming, coordinator of the Baptist Outreach Endeavour. We spoke on the phone. It's wonderful to have you as a member of our group."

Member of the group?

Scab wants to shrink back through the door, but Greg Fleming seizes his hand and pulls him in. He turns to the people in the room. "Ladies and gentlemen, please welcome our new friend, Julian Faye. He's working on a photo essay he calls *Night in the City.* He'd like to photograph our mission with the homeless."

The group applauds, smiling. There are twelve of them, men and women. They don't look like Baptist University students. Scab had a vague image in his head of monks and nuns, but the people in front of him are dressed in jeans and sweaters and fleece jackets and look like . . . well, students.

Greg Fleming grabs Scab's shoulder and pulls

him further into the room, saying, "Please join our fellowship while I finish my pre-mission talk."

Keeping his head down, Scab scuttles through the desks to the back of the room. A male student with neat black hair stands and holds out his hand. "I'm Jordan. Welcome. Have a seat," he says, his smooth complexion crinkling into a smile. He points to the desk beside him.

Scab sits.

From the front of the room, Greg Fleming booms, "Everyone is to meet back at the drop-off point at eleven. Julian, I'm assigning you to the team of Philomena and Jordan, since I see you have already made Jordan's acquaintance. Stay close to them at all times. And, finally, everyone, we'll go over the rules."

Jordan leans close to Scab and whispers, "Pastor Greg is very particular about his rules being observed."

The group leader goes on, "You will stay with your partner at all times. You will avoid any encounter that has the potential to turn violent or dangerous. You will offer no temptation to the people we set out to help. This means all jewellery, watches, rings, money, wallets, anything valuable, is to be left here, now. You can pick it up when we get back. Only one cell phone per team is allowed, and it is to be kept out of sight and used only in an emergency."

While he speaks, students pass a box around the room to put their valuables in. Pastor Greg nods at the cameras Scab has laid on the desk in front of him. "We'll make an exception for your cameras, of course. But be discreet."

Then he says to the group: "Let's say our usual prayer before we set out."

The students rise and form a circle at the front of the room, hands joined. Scab stays in his seat. Jordan looks back at him and waves him over.

You've got to be kidding, Scab thinks. He shakes his head.

"You are welcome to join our circle, Julian," Pastor Greg says. It is more of a command than an invitation.

Scab rises to his feet and stands awkwardly beside Jordan, who makes a space for him. Scab keeps his head down. Jordan grasps one of his hands, and he feels the other taken gently. He glances to that side. The young woman beside him smiles and whispers, "I'm Philomena. Welcome."

She's the same height as Scab, and instead of the jeans chosen by most of the group, she wears a short grey skirt and a light corduroy jacket with flowers embroidered on the sleeves. Her sneakers are tied with green laces.

Scab returns his gaze to the floor. He notices his breathing has quickened and he's sweating. Jordan and Philomena will feel it on his hands.

He hates this forced togetherness. He doesn't belong in this group; he doesn't belong in any group; he doesn't want to. He has nothing in common with these people. He has no faith like theirs, no burning desire to convert down-and-outers living on the street, no easy, confident manner like theirs.

He longs to bring the little camera to his eye to distance himself, but he's left it on the desk behind him. And anyway, his hands are now held firmly by his new partners.

Pastor Greg booms, "Lord, as we set out on our evening mission, help us in our endeavour to bring material and spiritual comfort to the unfortunate people we encounter, and at the same time, let our efforts bind us closer to you and to one another in our fellowship of service."

The students murmur "Amen," and file from the room. Scab follows them down the stairs and along a hallway to the rear of the building.

Jordan and Philomena are waiting for him outside.

"We have to stay together, so we may as well start now," says Jordan.

A passenger van, Atlantic Baptist University Outreach painted on its side, draws up. Pastor Greg is at the wheel. Philomena climbs in. Jordan stands back to let Scab enter. Philomena has settled herself in the rear seat, beside the window. Scab stops halfway down the van, looking for an empty seat. Philomena waves him to the place beside her. Jordan follows, and Scab finds himself jammed between them as two more students squeeze onto the end of the seat.

The van pulls out of the college gates.

Scab wishes he'd arranged to meet the group somewhere else, instead of travelling with them in this confined, intimate space. He feels himself shrinking from Philomena and Jordan, his shoulders hunching inwards, his legs pressing together, in a vain attempt not to touch, or be touched, by them. But the more he withdraws, the more they seem to press against him as the van lurches and sways. He is sweating again, and he's afraid he'll smell.

"There isn't much room, is there?" Philomena says suddenly. "Are you all right?"

He nods quickly.

The van stops in a line of traffic. A shuffling figure in a hooded sweatshirt, backpack hanging from one shoulder, is moving from vehicle to vehicle. The figure taps at window after window, and holds out a hand. Scab can't make out either the age or the sex of the panhandler. Most drivers ignore the figure. Some open the window a crack and hand out money.

When the panhandler reaches the van and taps at the window, Pastor Greg tells the student beside him in the front: "Open it."

The student opens the window.

Scab can see that the panhandler is a young man, about the same age as he is. He reaches out a hand. "Spare some change, eh?"

Pastor Greg leans across. "Why?"

"'Cos I got nothing to eat and nowhere to sleep."

"Like hell you haven't. Run along home to

mummy and daddy, clean yourself up, and stop giving the homeless a bad name."

The line of traffic begins to move. As Pastor Greg wheels the van forward, the young man peers through the window. He raises a finger and snarls, "Fucking do-gooders."

Pastor Greg mutters, "He's about as homeless and hungry as you and me."

Scab feels Philomena lean towards him. She exudes some kind of lemony scent. He glances up and finds their faces close to each other.

She whispers, "Pastor Greg can't stand fakes."

Scab frames her face mentally, as if sighting through his camera for a close-up portrait, noticing the smallness of her nose, which turns up at the end, and the smooth narrowness of her lips. Her hair, the colour of dark coffee, is parted at the centre and pulled back loosely behind her ears to hang in a ponytail. Her ochre eyes are level with his, and narrowed, as if sizing him up. Her skin is pockmarked, like she must have had a bad case of acne at some time.

He looks down quickly.

Philomena says, "I never introduced myself properly. I'm Philomena Pippy." She holds her hand out awkwardly in the cramped space. "May I call you Julian?"

Why should I care what you call me?

He shakes her hand. He's surprised at the firmness of her grip. "No one callsh me Julian anymore, except my parentsh."

Why did I say that?

"What do your friends call you?"

My friends — right.

"Sh-shcab."

She laughs. "Why 'Scab'?"

Leave me alone.

He mumbles, "The kidsh at shchool shay becaushe I'm irritating and annoying and ugly like a shcab."

Shit. The lisp.

"I'll call you Julian."

"You may ash well jusht call me Shcab. I'm ushed to it."

. . . .

8:45 P.M.
JUNCTION OF CITY AND WATERLOO

Pastor Greg pulls up near the corner of City and Waterloo. The students gather at the rear of the van. Jordan opens the doors, revealing a stack of neatly folded blankets and a pile of backpacks. Philomena tucks a few blankets under her arm, while Jordan throws a backpack over his shoulder. They explain to Scab, "We carry bottles of water, a thermos of tea, a first-aid kit, and a bit of food, as well as the blankets."

Pastor Greg, directing the group, tells Jordan and Philomena, "Check out the alleys off the side streets."

Jordan and Philomena set off along City Road, past an assortment of cafés, bars, and corner stores that serve the housing developments and apartment blocks nearby. Scab hangs back, checking the settings on his cameras. He's got the ISO as high as possible because he doesn't want to use flash. The white balance is on auto, colour at "faithful" although he'll probably print in black and white. The aperture is wide to give as fast a shutter speed as possible, frames to be saved as raw files. All sounds turned off to minimize the chance of causing a distraction.

Satisfied, he slings the big camera over his shoulder, tucking it out of sight behind him. He holds the little one in the palm of his hand, low and inconspicuous, but ready to shoot.

Philomena looks back. "Coming?" she calls to him.

"I'll follow."

He forces himself to move through the evening crowds of pedestrians cruising the sidewalk. He misses nothing:

A boisterous group of hockey fans on their way to a game;

A woman pushing a hand cart piled with bulging grocery bags;

Four teenage girls giggling and falling against one another.

Jordan and Philomena stop under a streetlight. They look out of place, hair and clothes too neat, faces too fresh. They are too obviously on a mission. He photographs them, aiming the little camera without raising it.

Despite his caution, one of the hockey fans notices and calls, "Hey — you. Why don't you take my picture?" and strikes a pose.

Scab pretends not to hear. He fingers the little can of WD40 he always carries in his pocket. He's never had to use it, but he likes to know it's there.

A quick shot of oil in the face. Enough time to get away.

The hockey fan shouts louder, "Hey, you, Mr. Photographer. Take my picture." He staggers sideways into his companions as he attempts a new pose. There's a scuffle as they shove him away.

Scab takes the opportunity to quickly move on. He follows his partners onto a side street. A sign says "Cedar Lane" but there aren't any cedars. They pass a row of once-elegant townhouses, most now rundown. Some show signs of renovation, their tiny front yards boasting new walkways of coloured stone, shrubs planted optimistically between the paths.

They come to a small, square apartment block. In the dirt parking lot beside it, a pile of abandoned children's toys lies in a corner. Scab stops to photograph the toys.

A rusting yellow dump truck.

Leaning goal posts without a net.

A bicycle on its side, with training wheels sticking up.

A doll without a head.

They come to another row of townhouses, these converted to apartments. They have leaning steps that lead to sagging verandas housing old couches. Music blares from an upstairs window. The streetlights are spaced so far apart here that pools of blackness lie between them.

Scab trails further behind Jordan and Philomena as he photographs. He uses the big camera now, trying to capture his companions under one of the lights, silhouetted against the decrepit cityscape.

Philomena and Jordan turn between the narrow houses into a back alley. Peering into the shadows, Scab sees his partners have stopped.

He stops, too.

He watches as Jordan swings the backpack from his shoulder, and Philomena leans down, reaching towards a shape on the ground. Scab creeps closer. The shape becomes a person. Jordan squats, opening the pack. Philomena kneels, speaking softly.

Scab searches for light — any light — to illuminate the scene. There's a streetlight at the far end of the alley, where it connects to another street.

Scab slinks past his partners and crouches against a wire mesh fence at the side of the lane, sighting the big camera on the group. The shape on the ground sits up, revealing itself as an old man or woman — he can't tell which — bulky in thick clothing.

"Would you like some tea?" he hears Philomena ask.

The shape props itself on one elbow and demands, "Why?"

A woman, Scab decides.

"To warm you."

"I'll be pissing in my sleep if I drink anything. I don't wake up when I need to go, not no more. Who're you?"

"We're from the Baptist Outreach Mission."

"Why'd you wake me?"

"To see if there's anything you need."

"Water, or a blanket?" Jordan suggests.

Scab is taking pictures of Philomena and Jordan as they kneel on either side of the woman.

"What the hell would I want a blanket for?" she demands.

"To be comfortable."

"Blankets make me sweat. Then I stink."

"We have some food," suggests Philomena.

"I eat already."

"Do you want anything?"

"I want to sleep. Why do you keep bothering me?"

"Sorry." Philomena rises and tucks the blankets back under her arm. "God bless you," she says, and sets off, Jordan beside her.

Scab lets them pass. He looks back. The woman is sitting up, watching. She sees Scab and raises her middle finger.

He takes the picture.

He follows Jordan and Philomena to the end of the alley, where they emerge onto Pine Boulevard.

No pine trees either.

The lights here seem even more widely spaced than on Cedar, and the pools of darkness bigger. His partners plunge into another narrow alley. Scab follows and finds himself in almost complete darkness. He waits for his eyes to adjust, then makes out a flickering light ahead.

A man's voice, raucous and hoarse, shouts, "Motorists will drive on the right hand side of the road. Pedestrians will keep to the sidewalk, unless they have to cross the street, and then they will do so at designated crossings."

Scab grins. Road Safety Charlie.

At the same time he thinks he hears, beneath Charlie's rant, the sound of weeping. He listens. The sound has stopped.

Did it even exist in the first place?

A woman's husky voice calls out, "Take your nonsense somewhere else, Charlie."

Road Safety Charlie appears in the light, one hand demonstrating the actions he describes.

"Halt!" His hand is raised.

"Proceed!" A sweeping motion.

"Keep to the right!" One finger pointing.

Scab smiles as he captures it all. *He should be called Hand Jive Charlie,* he thinks.

The woman groans, "Will someone shut him up, for Christ's sake?" She falls into a fit of coughing.

Charlie starts again, lurching towards the woman's voice. "Icy conditions make driving treacherous."

Jordan slips the backpack from his shoulder and moves quickly forward. "Come on, Charlie. We've heard it all before."

Philomena takes the backpack and moves closer to the flickering light so she can see inside the bag. Scab sneaks forward until he can see into the lighted area.

The alley is a dead end. Two candles flicker at the back of the space, faintly illuminating what Scab makes out to be the entry to an old garage. It's littered with boxes, newspapers, and chunks of rusted metal, like old machine parts. A shape, a woman, is lying on the ground beside the candles. Philomena kneels beside her.

From the corner of his eye, Scab sees Jordan, further along the alley, put his hand on Charlie's arm. Charlie shakes himself free and starts kicking the high wooden fence that runs along one side of the lane.

Someone in one of the houses backing on to the alley shouts, "Shut the fuck up or I'm calling the police!"

Philomena, leaning over the woman, says, "Try to breathe deeply."

The woman supports herself on one elbow, still coughing.

Scab has lurked in doorways photographing the night long enough to recognize a volatile situation.

Charlie shouts, "Shut the fuck up yourself."

Jordan tries to restrain him. They wrestle.

Scab glances back at Philomena and the

woman. There is barely enough light for shooting, but the image is too good not to try. The young woman, kneeling to cradle the destitute woman with the drawn, haggard face, her mouth gaping and her lips curling outwards as she coughs.

Scab kneels, bracing himself with his shoulder against the fence to hold the camera steady as he frames the two women. Without moving the camera, he shifts focus to watch Jordan and Charlie. Jordan is holding Charlie in a bear hug, but Charlie frees his fist and shakes it, ranting, "All cars must display their registration stickers in the appropriate place."

"I said shut the fuck up!" The same voice as before.

"Check your tire pressures weekly," Charlie yells.

"Oh, for Christ's sake. I'm calling the police." A window slams shut.

Charlie pulls himself free of Jordan. He takes off in the direction of the complaining voice, gesticulating and shouting, "While the driver's handbook is an advisory, not a legal document, its contents nevertheless reflect the law as it applies to all road users."

Jordan runs after him. "Be quiet, Charlie, or the police will take you in again," he urges.

Charlie suddenly turns and pushes Jordan, hard, sending him reeling against the fence. Jordan pushes himself off the fence and tries to grab him, but Charlie, laughing, dances just out of reach. As Jordan lunges again, Charlie takes off running down the alley. Jordan glances back to where Philomena is tending the woman. "I have to stop him before he does something stupid," he calls, and sets off in pursuit.

Scab turns his attention back to Philomena. He squeezes the shutter halfway and waits while the lens searches for focus in the dim light. As he checks the perimeter of the viewfinder to make sure there is nothing unnecessary in the frame, he makes out another figure moving quietly from the shadowy corner of the garage.

A long coat, a woollen cap pulled low, moving towards Philomena.

The Crying Man — not crying.

He hasn't noticed Scab, who is still kneeling on the other side of the alley. Scab looks back at Philomena, and sees what has attracted the Crying Man. A thin silver necklace gleams in the candlelight.

Something on the Crying Man gleams too.

Knife! Scab silently warns.

Still watching through the viewfinder, Scab sees Philomena lay the woman down gently and straighten up.

The Crying Man freezes.

Philomena reaches into her pocket and pulls out a tissue. She leans forward again, cradles the woman, and wipes her face. She's unaware of the man in the shadows, who starts towards her again, one hand reaching towards the necklace, the other gripping the knife.

I should shout to her, Scab thinks, then lets it all play out in his head like a scene from a movie. *I rush forward and throw myself between Philomena and her attacker, risk getting myself injured and my cameras broken.*

But the scene he is shooting with his camera is better. In the viewfinder is a stunning trinity.

The Sufferer.

The Saviour.

The Spoiler.

He shoots several frames, then thinks, *Now I'll stop it somehow.*

With one hand he feels for the WD40 in his pocket. But his eye is still to the camera. The balance of the photo isn't quite right. The Crying Man needs to be slightly closer to Philomena and the woman.

Just one more shot . . .

But when the Crying Man advances again, his step is longer than the one before, and now he's too close.

Shit.

Scab shifts position and reframes it.

Charlie's voice comes faintly from the street. "Canada's level of road safety during 1998, as measured by road users killed per registered motor vehicle, improved by almost nine percent since the country adopted a national road safety vision in 1996."

"Shut up, Charlie, or so help me, I'll let the police deal with you," warns Jordan.

Damn you, Jordan, Scab thinks. *It shouldn't be my job to help your partner, especially when you've both broken Pastor Greg's rules — you by not staying with your partner, Philomena by not removing the necklace.*

The Crying Man shrinks back a little.

There! Scab thinks. But at the same time Philomena moves her face, casting a shadow across it, while the light still falls on the woman and the Crying Man. Scab keeps shooting. Philomena is bound to move her face back into the soft light, and the Crying Man isn't moving. There's still time.

One more frame, he decides, *with the light falling across Philomena's face, and then I'll shout a warning.*

Philomena wipes the woman's forehead again. The woman looks up at her, the trace of a smile forcing its way through her coughing. The light catches both their faces. At the same time the Crying Man inches forward. He raises the hand holding the knife, raising his face with it, so that the light falls across it harder and harsher, turning his face into a mask of horror. Scab shoots three quick frames.

Charlie's voice is even farther away now: "Failure to comply with advice given in the driver's handbook will not, in itself, cause a person to be prosecuted . . . however, it may be used to establish liability .. ."

And Jordan is closer now. "To hell with you

then, Charlie." His voice suddenly stronger, more urgent. "Philomena? Are you okay?"

The Crying Man lunges for the necklace.

Philomena looks up at him. Screams.

The knife slashes her face as the Crying Man tears the necklace from her throat. She reaches to grab it back. He swings it away from her and her hand grabs at his coat instead. She holds on, pulling him down. He falls on her.

Scab runs across the alley to them, clutching the big camera to his chest and pulling the WD40 from his pocket. The Crying Man pushes himself off Philomena and lurches into Scab's path. Scab manages to spray oil in his face before he collides with him. The Crying Man is more solid than Scab expects, and retreats only a step before staggering forward, one hand pawing at his eyes, the other flailing blindly with the knife. Scab feels the blade graze his cheek as he flings himself sideways to avoid him. He trips over Philomena.

The Crying Man disappears into the blackness of the alley.

"What's happened?" Jordan says, running over to them. He sees Scab and says, "Christ." He pulls out his cell phone.

Scab feels blood trickling into his mouth. He's fallen half across Philomena. He pushes himself off her and mumbles, "Philomena needs an ambulance."

"One injured," Jordan yells into the phone. He corrects himself: "Two injured . . . maybe three. A woman . . . seems to have fainted . . . No, her face is bloody. Jesus, Philomena . . ." Jordon lets his voice trail off and lowers his phone.

"Don't move," he says as he bends over her. He pulls the first-aid kit from the backpack and digs into it. He's holding a wad of gauze against Philomena's cheek with one hand when he and Scab notice the blood seeping through her jacket, just below her ribs.

Without hesitation, Jordon tears open her jacket and lifts her T-shirt. Scab glimpses her bra as he forces himself to look down at the bloody wound low in Philomena's side. Jordan grabs more gauze and presses it against the cut.

The homeless woman, between coughs, says, "It'd be nice to have some peace around here."

. . . .

10:50 P.M.
REGIONAL HOSPITAL
Scab surveys himself in the washroom mirror. He carefully peels the dressing from his cheek. The knife cut, only a few centimetres long, has stopped bleeding. He throws the bandage into the garbage. He told the ambulance attendants he was okay, but they insisted not only on dressing the cut, but also on taking him in the ambulance with Philomena. She opened her eyes only once during the ride, smiled at him, and whispered, "Thank you."

Now he's in ER at the Regional Hospital. He doesn't know where they've taken Philomena. A nurse has looked at his wound and given him a shot. She told him the doctor would want to see him before he was allowed to leave.

What's to stop me from just walking out?

It's nearly 11 P.M. His assignment is done for the night, and he wants to get home and download his pictures.

Scab leaves the washroom, crosses the waiting room quickly, and peers into the hallway. The exit is a few metres to his right. A few metres to his left, he sees Pastor Greg and Jordan standing outside a room. Their heads are bent low with a man and a woman who look as if they just stepped out of a Gap commercial. He hears the man say, "Our Philomena," and guesses they are her parents.

Pastor Greg and Jordan have their backs to Scab. He sidles towards the exit. He's about to slip outside, when he hears Pastor Greg's booming voice. "Mr. Faye! We need to talk to you!"

Scab scuttles outside and runs for the bus.

. . . .

11:40 P.M.
FARM CRESCENT

Mrs. Faye appears from the kitchen in her dressing gown. "You're late!"

Scab has just opened the door. "For what?"

"Don't smart-mouth me, young man. It's nearly midnight."

"So?"

"Your father and I have been worrying about you." She calls into the living room behind her.

"Haven't we, Gorman?"

No answer.

She looks more closely at Scab as he steps into the light in the hallway. "You're hurt!"

"It's just a little cut."

"What happened?"

"Nothing."

"Does it hurt?"

"Nah."

"Shall I put a bandage on it for you?"

"I'm okay."

He sets off upstairs.

"Would you like a snack?"

"Nah. Thanks. I have to work on my pictures."

"You're going to work — at this hour of the night! You'll overtire yourself."

He closes his door firmly and sits at the computer to download the night's pictures. He's impatient to see whether the frames of Philomena and the Crying Man are as good as he thinks. He scrolls through the early-evening scenes until, at last, he reaches the scenes from the dead-end alley.

There's Philomena, kneeling beside the woman, soothing her as she's wracked by coughs.

And there's the Crying Man, ready to attack. The camera caught him even before Scab was aware of his presence.

Scab scrolls through the images.

He hopes he didn't miss the moment he foresaw, the moment when the balance between evil and compassion was perfectly poised. He scrolls some more.

Here it is.

The trinity of the kneeling Madonna, the anguished woman, and the mysterious attacker. Twin lights gleaming on necklace and knife, uniting both objects and their owners.

He changes the picture to black and white, lightens the shadows just a little, and throws a weak spotlight on Philomena's face to heighten the angelic, otherworldly quality of it.

Brilliant.

* * *

Eight o'clock Saturday morning, Scab calls the *Chronicle* and describes the picture to the news editor.

"Sounds interesting," he replies. "Why don't you drop it off sometime in the next few days, and maybe we'll take a look."

Scab puts the phone down and mutters, "Stupid fuck."

He calls Mr. Rent. He answers the phone after only one ring. "What?"

"Sorry if I woke you."

"What have you got?"

"Only the best picture ever."

"I hope so for your sake, disturbing my beauty sleep like this."

"It is."

71

"Did you call the news editor?"

"He said to drop it off sometime in the next few days."

"Okay. You better send it to me, then."

Scab e-mails the picture to Mr. Rent.

He calls back a few minutes later. "It's good. Save it on disc. I'll be around in a few minutes to pick it up and take it in. After we use it, I'll get my agency to send it out. I might even submit it for the Young Photographer of the Year contest. You okay with that?"

"Sure. Whatever."

MONDAY, JUNE 22ND

9:23 A.M.
HARBOURSIDE HIGH SCHOOL

All Scab wants to do is sidle into school for the last time, clean out his locker, collect a few of his things — a sweater, a pair of sneakers, some pens — and leave. But from the moment he arrives, everyone seems to be looking at him.

As he walks down the hallway, he sees students and teachers nudging one another and nodding in his direction. It's like he's the only one not in on some secret.

Brett Hanley, surrounded by the usual crowd of girls, sneers, "So you finally climbed out of the slime and made a name for yourself, Julie Scab."

Scab, fingering the little camera, ignores him.

He slinks into homeroom, hoping it'll be empty.

It's not. Mr. Kinney is there. The teacher jumps up, seizes Scab's hand, and shakes it vigorously.

"Congratulations. I thought your pictures of the fire were good, but your latest is . . . is . . . is a work of art."

"Wha—"

"Your photograph — from Friday night . . ."

Scab shrugs, mystified.

"Don't tell me you haven't seen the newspaper."

Scab shakes his head. His parents don't get the *Chronicle* delivered. Mr. Faye always brings one home from the mill. So the only time Scab sees it is late in the evening, when his father has finished with it, or when he's at the newspaper office. When he first had photographs in the *Chronicle*, he used to rush out and buy one as soon as it hit the stands. Now it's old hat, he doesn't bother.

Mr. Kinney takes a copy from his desk and unfolds it. Scab's picture of Philomena, the old woman, and the Crying Man fills most of the front page, leaving room only for the headline above the picture, and a caption below.

DANGER STALKS ANGEL OF MERCY

Chronicle photographer Julian Faye rescued Ms. Philomena Pippy, a young

Baptist University Outreach Endeavour volunteer on a mission to help the homeless, seconds after this photograph was taken, an action that Pastor Greg Fleming, leader of the group, describes as "selfless and heroic." (For full story see page A3)

Photo by Julian Faye, *Saint John Chronicle*

"Shit," Scab mutters. He imagines a picture of himself on the front page. He can think of nothing worse than having his anonymity taken away like this.

He catches himself. *Why did I boast to Mr. Rent that it was my best picture ever if I didn't want to get it "out there"?*

Mr. Kinney says, "Don't talk like that when you're with the principal, will you?"

Scab looks at him, frowning, mystified again.

"Didn't you hear the announcement?"

Scab was vaguely aware of the usual babbling over the PA when he got to school, but blotted it out like he always did. He shakes his head.

"The principal congratulated you on the photograph and on your actions," Mr. Kinney explains. "He said you'd brought honour and pride to the school, and that an emergency meeting of the awards committee had been held. You've been selected as this year's recipient of the Outstanding Achievement in Art award! He also told the whole school that your achievements in

photography were an example to all of how
personal adversity could be overcome in the
pursuit of extraordinary achievement."

Mr. Kinney beams.

"Pershonal adsverhity?"

"Why, yes. You've achieved remarkable
success despite being — how can I put it? —
unsociable, and having a speech . . . uh . . .
problem. That's all the principal meant. Anyway,
at the end of his announcement, he asked you to
report to his office right away. I expect he wants
to congratulate you in person. You'd better get
down there."

Scab nods and heads for the door.

Mr. Kinney calls after him. "Hey — I meant
what I said. You've got hundreds — thousands —
of people, not just at school, but all over the city,
admiring your work. And I'm one of them," he
adds.

Scab nods again.

Ms. Sanders, the girls' phys. ed. teacher, is on
duty in the hallway. She marches up to Scab and
seizes his hand in both of hers. "Mr. Faye,
congratulations on your picture, and on your
bravery. You're a fine example of what a man —
a *gentle*man — should be!"

Scab mumbles, "Thanks," and makes his way
down the hallway, past more stares. An image of
the bloody slash across Philomena's cheek flits
through his mind. He runs his fingertips over the
small cut on his own cheek. Lowering his hand

from his face, he notes with satisfaction the trace of blood on his fingers.

At the end of the hall, the principal's office is to the right, the exit left. Scab veers left and feels a hand on his shoulder. He looks around.

Mr. Kinney grins. "I thought you might have difficulty finding your way. You'd best see the principal — really."

He ushers Scab into the office and calls to the secretary, "Ms. Young, here's Julian to see Mr. Wood."

Ms. Young is short and broad-shouldered. "Oh, Julian," she coos. "I was just reading the article about your heroics of the other night and admiring your wonderful photograph."

Scab half-turns in a final attempt to escape, but Mr. Kinney bars his way. "Hold on — you're bleeding. Best clean yourself up before you go in," he says.

Ms. Young produces a tissue and dabs gently at Scab's cheek, saying, "Does it hurt, dear?" She steps back to inspect her work and nods, satisfied.

"Mr. Wood, here's Julian, our very own hero," she announces, knocking at an inner door.

She pushes the door fully open, revealing the principal seated behind his desk. Sitting opposite him is Pastor Greg.

"Our shy hero!" Pastor Greg says, as both men stand.

"You're a strange one, Julian Faye. You've hardly said a word to anyone since you arrived at

Harbourside High," says Mr. Wood.

Because every time I spoke, someone made fun of me, Scab thinks.

"You've cruised through your high-school career without causing a ripple in academics or sports or anything else. Now, suddenly, just when we're about to lose you, we discover you're not only an artist, but also a hero." He chuckles as he sits back behind his desk. "Julian Faye, we hardly knew you."

You never tried.

Pastor Greg sits, too, and Mr. Wood waves Scab to a chair. "Well — say something!"

Scab stays standing.

"I'm the sh-same I've alwaysh been."

The lisp.

"Pastor Greg is here to offer his congratulations. I gather you didn't give him time to the other night."

"He was too modest even to allow the lady he rescued to thank him," says Pastor Greg.

The principal goes on, "Pastor Greg had to track you down with a call to the newspaper. He has a job for you. What classes do you have this morning? Math and English — right? I don't think the teachers will mind if you miss them at this stage of the year. I've already spoken to your parents, and they're happy for you to accompany Pastor Greg."

"Where?"

"To the hospital, of course. So the young lady

can thank you properly." Mr. Wood rises to shake Scab's hand again. "Congratulations on your work and your bravery. The school is proud of you."

"Philomena begged me to find you. She so desperately wants to thank you for saving her," Pastor Greg explains, also rising.

"I didn't sh-sh-save her."

His fingers itch to probe at his cut again.

Pastor Greg and Mr. Wood look at one another, smiling, and Mr. Wood says, "Still the shy hero!"

Pastor Greg escorts Scab through the empty school halls and outside to his car. As they drive to the hospital, Scab digs his fingers into the cut on his face again, until they come away bloody.

He looks at them with satisfaction.

. . . .

10:00 A.M.
REGIONAL HOSPITAL

Pastor Greg says, "I'll show you to Philomena's room."

You're afraid I'll take off unless you deliver me there, Scab thinks.

At the door, Pastor Greg knocks quietly, then says, "I'll leave the two of you alone."

He pushes Scab inside, and closes the door behind him.

Philomena is sitting up in bed. A thick pad of gauze is held against her right cheek with a bandage that is wrapped right around her head. Her left eye is black. A vase on the bedside table holds a large bouquet of flowers. A card poking out of it reads: *For our brave girl. Love, Mom and Dad*. Another, smaller bunch contains the card: *Jordan. XX*.

Scab hovers by the door. He wonders whether Philomena has seen her picture on the front page and looks around furtively for the *Chronicle*. He can't see it.

She says, "Come closer."

He shuffles forward a few steps.

"I said closer, silly. I won't bite."

He takes two more cautious steps into the room. She seizes his hand and pulls him forward so that he stumbles and falls towards the bed. He puts his hands on each side of her to stop himself falling on her. She wraps her arms around his neck and says, "Thank you."

He pushes himself free. "For nothing."

"For saving me, dummy."

For not warning you . . .

"What happened to you that night? I wanted to thank you then."

. . . for not stopping him . . .

"I had to get home."

. . . for thinking more of getting a good picture than of what might happen to you . . .

"You were injured, too."

. . . for letting them all think I'm a hero when I'm not . . .

"Nah. It'sh nothing."

Shit. The lisp. Making me sound stupid, as usual.

Maybe he should tell her everything. Let her scorn and anger replace the scorn he feels for himself. Maybe she'd punch him. He hopes she'd aim for the cut on his cheek; make it bleed some more.

She reaches up and brushes her fingertips against his wound. He flinches. She says, "Sorry. Is it painful?"

He lies. "A bit." Then adds, stupidly, "You've got a black eye."

"I think he hit me with his shoulder when he fell against me."

I could have stopped that from happening, too.

She gestures towards a chair by the bed. "Why don't you sit for a few minutes?"

"Why?"

He can feel the tension rising in him. That means the lisp is about to get worse, and he'll sound even more pathetic.

She laughs. "It's what you do when you visit someone in hospital." As if reading his mind, she goes on, "You don't have to say anything. You can just sit and I'll do the talking. I'm good at it." Scab still hangs back and she pleads, "Sit . . . please?"

He obeys.

She starts, "Well — here we are. You don't mind if I call you Scab, do you? You said it was okay, but I'll call you Julian, if you prefer . . ." She giggles. "Or Mr. Faye . . ."

She looks at him.

"Sh-Sh-Shcab's okay."

"Good. What was I saying? Yes — Here we are ... Scab ... you and me, at the hospital, both with cuts on our faces, and me with a black eye, too. Oh, and a cut on my stomach. Hey, how did you get off school, anyway? Do you have permission? I suppose Pastor Greg made it okay. He's good at getting what he wants. But not with the Outreach group, not where money's concerned. He told us at the meeting before we went out that night that the group's in financial trouble and may have to cut back on its activities. It's true. We've just about run out of money, and there's no more coming in. That reminds me — why don't you come to one of our meetings, not to take pictures, but just to be part of the group? You'll like it — you wouldn't have to say anything — and I'd like you to come. How am I doing?"

"Wh-what?"

"How am I doing — doing all the talking so you don't have to?" She grins at him. "That wasn't so bad, was it? I mean visiting me in hospital."

He manages a brief grin in return. "Shorry."

"You shouldn't say sorry so much. You've nothing to be sorry for."

He glances at the bandage wrapped around her face and wonders what she'll look like when it comes off.

Is she scarred for life? Permanently disfigured?

He has an urge to tell her everything now. To

get it over with. To accept her anger. To never see her again.

He clears his throat. "You know that picture . . . thoshe picturesh . . . I was-sh taking the night it happened?"

"Oh yes. How did they come out?"

So she hasn't seen the Chronicle.

"Okay. But when I was-sh taking them . . ." He searches for the words for his confession.

I saw the Crying Man creeping up on you, but I didn't bother to say anything.

I saw the Crying Man stalking you, but decided getting a good picture was worth more than you getting disfigured for life.

She prompts, "When you were taking them . . ."

I could have warned you — should have warned you.

He hears voices in the hallway. Pastor Greg's and someone else's. There's a knock at the door. Scab stands and moves towards it.

"It's just my parents," Philomena says. "You don't have to go."

The door opens slowly and cautiously.

"Hi, Sweetie," a woman says, peeking her head around the door. "Can we come in?"

Why shouldn't you come in? Scab thinks. *What do you think we're doing in here, making out?*

He feels himself blush at the thought.

"'Course you can come in, Mom. What do you think we're doing in here —?" Philomena says, echoing his thoughts.

She looks at Scab as she speaks, and he feels his blush deepen. She grins.

The door opens further, and Scab quickly moves behind it. Philomena's mom marches to the bed and embraces her. A man follows her into the room and stands at the end of the bed. He's holding a copy of the *Chronicle*. Scab slips outside.

He hears Philomena say, "This is Scab . . . Julian . . . who rescued me. Scab, this is . . . Scab?"

Pastor Greg is hovering outside the room.

Scab mumbles, "I have to go to the bathroom," and takes off down the hallway.

Outside the hospital, he makes his way to the bus stop. The #67 that would take him past the high school is loading. He starts to jog towards it, but stops. He has no good reason to go back to school. He could care less about his stuff. Someone else can clear out his locker and toss his sweaters and sneakers. Instead he decides to head straight down to the *Chronicle*. Today is his last day of co-op.

He waits for the downtown bus.

. . . .

11:55 A.M.
MARKET SLIP, DOWNTOWN
Scab gets off the bus near the waterfront. Almost immediately he spots the Crying Man. He is silent, staring at the sparkling ripples on the harbour, just as he was silent the night he stared at Philomena's necklace.

Am I supposed to be angry with him, for such a heartless attack?

Am I supposed to want revenge?

Or am I supposed to just pity his instability and confusion and loneliness . . . And thank him for getting me such a great picture?

When the police arrived shortly after the ambulance on the night of the attack, Scab had been surprised at first by Pastor Greg's insistence that they not go after the attacker. They'd asked Scab if he knew the man and, catching Pastor Greg's eye, he lied, saying that he'd never seen him before and didn't think he'd recognize him either, because it was so dark and everything happened so quickly.

Later, just before he went in the ambulance, Pastor Greg whispered, "You know him, don't you?" When Scab nodded, Pastor Greg said, "Good man."

Pastor Greg had asked Jordan why the man had attacked Philomena. Jordan, also catching Scab's eye, said, "Maybe he was after the supplies . . ."

Scab takes a last look at the Crying Man before moving away to buy coffee from a street vendor. Now that the picture has made the front page of the paper, he knows it won't be long until the police figure it out and come looking for him.

The harbour is still, and the heads of two seals bob in the water in front of him. He decides to walk to the *Chronicle*. He'll be early, but it doesn't matter. It's warm and sunny and the benches scattered around the gardens on King

Square are filled with tourists and office workers. As he wanders across the grass, he wonders why he can't imagine himself part of a group, enjoying its banter and camaraderie. Why did he shy away from everyone?

I like being alone, he tells himself firmly.

So why does he feel a kind of sad loneliness when he watches the closeness of others, like the people here, and like Philomena and Jordan and their friends in the Outreach group?

He wonders how they see him. As proudly detached and aloof — or pathetically alone and friendless?

How could I help being friendless when I've been taunted my whole life?

So why, then, did Philomena invite him to join the Outreach group? *Pity?*

She was the one needing pity now. For the disfigurement she has to live with; the scar he didn't save her from. Scab catches sight of his reflection in a store window. The cut on his cheek is bleeding heavily. He hadn't realized he was picking at it again.

. . . .

12:25 P.M.
CROWN STREET

Foster Rent is driving out of the *Chronicle* parking lot as Scab arrives.

"Scab, my man. Congratulations on getting your first front page! The paper had a call about it

86

this morning, before I was in. Someone calling himself Pastor Greg. Said he was the leader of the group you were photographing and wanted to know how he could contact you. Said you took off before he or the girl could thank you for doing the hero bit. The news editor told him to call the school. Hope that was okay."

"He didn't just call the school. He showed up there."

"And you didn't run away from him again?"

Scab grins. "Thought about it."

"But you spoke to him — right?"

"Yeah. He wanted to make a big deal out of the other night. Wanted me to see the girl."

"Did you?"

"He took me to the hospital."

"How'd you make out there?"

"What do you mean?"

"I mean with you not being Mr. Socialite of the Year. Did you at least manage to have a conversation with the girl?"

"I guessh."

"Good. And you're going to visit her again, I suppose."

"Nah."

"Why not? She's cute, isn't she? And she'll feel she owes you, you being her knight in shining armour. Take advantage." He winks before adding, "There's nothing on the agenda for this afternoon, so I'm taking off. They can call me if anything comes up. You can take off, too, if you like. I won't tell the school." He grins. "Like it'd bother you if I did. Got anywhere to go?"

"Nah."

"Just don't hang around downtown, will you. It'd make us look bad."

The car starts moving forward again, then stops. "You're welcome to hang out at my place. We can talk about photography. That way you'll still be doing your co-op. Sort of."

. . . .

12:40 P.M.
HARBOURFRONT APARTMENTS

Scab gazes out the big picture window in Mr. Rent's apartment. It's on Water Street in a converted warehouse. Shops, bars, and restaurants are on the lower floor, and apartments are above. Only the street and the harbourside trail lie between the building and the Saint John harbour. Scab watches as the Nova Scotia ferry sets out from the terminal on the other side. Half a dozen fishing boats are tied at an old wharf, while a cruise ship, one of the first of the season, makes its slow way into the harbour, escorted by a trio of tugboats. Mr. Rent's window will be level with the cruise ship's first tier of cabins when the ship berths at the terminal. The higher tiers will tower above the old warehouse and many of the other downtown buildings, making everything look out of proportion.

The first time Scab was in this apartment,

Mr. Rent talked about "seeing," never even mentioning cameras or photography. He stood at the apartment window, pointing in different directions. Fishing boats and an oil tanker waiting to come into port. Hikers on the trail.

"What do you see?" he'd asked Scab.

"A man walking his dog," Scab had offered.

Mr. Rent had scoffed at his timid observation. It had been his first experience of how demanding his mentor could be. He remembers the conversation almost word for word. Mr. Rent, exasperated, demanding, "What do you *really* see?"

Scab repeating, even more timidly, "Jusht a man walking his dog."

"What sort of dog?"

"A big one. A German shepherd, I think."

"What's the man holding?"

"Er — flowersh."

"Would you take a bunch of flowers with you if you were walking your dog?"

"Guessh not."

"How's the man dressed?"

"Sportsh jacket. Dressh pants. Shirt. Sh-sort of good, I guessh."

Scab was so nervous his lisp was out of control.

"Would you dress nicely to walk the dog?"

"Guessh not."

"So what do you really see?"

"A man with a dog . . . er . . . on hish way to meet shomeone . . . shomeone he'sh dressed up for . . . hish girlfriend!"

Mr. Rent pointed further along the trail. "There she is."

"She's got a dog, too. A little white poodle."

"Tell me when the picture happens."

The man and woman embraced.

"Now!" Scab suggested.

"Too soon. See what develops."

As the couple embraced, the German shepherd clumsily mounted the poodle.

Scab and Mr. Rent had laughed, Mr. Rent saying, "There's your picture. There's always a story, wherever you look. If it's not happening, it's about to. You have to look — *really* look — and keep looking. You have to *see*."

The apartment was new then.

Scab looks around.

It's still as tidy as ever. Not that there's much to keep clean. It's little more than a big room, sparsely furnished with two easy chairs, a big flat-screen TV and sound system, and a desk with a computer. The floors are bare hardwood, and the walls are lined with photographs.

Mr. Rent reaches into the cupboard under the counter. "I'm having a drink." He grins at Scab. "And you're not. But you're welcome to a soda."

Scab shakes his head.

While Mr. Rent pours a scotch, Scab walks around the room, looking at the photographs he's seen hundreds of times. Several are from Vietnam. Beside them a plaque: World Press Photo Award. Another plaque, this one reading "Robert Capa

Gold Medal," hangs beside a photograph of a Vietnamese woman weeping over a dead man, huts and army trucks and soldiers in the background.

There are no family photographs, and only one of Mr. Rent. He's standing with his cameras around his neck, bombed-out buildings behind him. *Beirut 1976* is scribbled at the bottom. He doesn't seem to have changed much since then. He's still thin, with slightly hunched shoulders, and the same thick hair, grey even then, flopping across his forehead. It's the same narrowed eyes, as if he's always squinting into the sun. In the photograph his face is lined, as it is now, but the scar isn't there, the livid mark on the side of his chin where a bullet had grazed him as it deflected off one of the cameras hanging around his neck. He told Scab once that the bullet had been meant for him.

Among the Vietnam pictures, there's one of a young girl. It stands out from the scenes of war and suffering. It's posed, the girl in half-profile, standing against a dark background. The only illumination is a shaft of light falling softly on her face. Her eyes are fixed on the photographer. Scab thinks she's about his own age. She looks both sad and beautiful. Once he'd asked Mr. Rent who she was. "Just someone I met over there," he had answered curtly. Scab never mentioned the picture again.

As Mr. Rent pours himself another scotch, he says, "By the way, congratulations on upsetting the Minister for Social Welfare."

Scab looks at him, puzzled.

"The minister's aide asked you to take some pictures of her highness working selflessly among the homeless."

"Oh. Yeah."

"And you walked out."

"Right."

"The minister is a friend of our esteemed editor. He asked me about the incident."

"Shorry."

"Don't be. I told him it's not our job to make politicians look good."

He turns on the stereo and a repeated riff of slow swooping sounds fills the apartment.

Mr. Rent sits and swivels his chair so that he can look out across the harbour. "So, Scab, my man," he says. "It's been a privilege — really — having you do the co-op thing at the *Chronicle*. I'm sorry it's coming to an end, but I'm happy you'll be around for the summer. Where do you see yourself two years from now, when you finish your course at Loyalist?"

Scab takes the other chair. "Looking for work, I suppose."

"You won't have to look for work. You'll have newspapers, maybe even magazines, lining up to take you on. You can work at the *Chronicle* if you like — I'll get you a job — though I hope I'll be retired by then. But it'd be better for you to get away."

"I want to freelance. Do my own stuff."

"Sure. But you have to start somewhere, get a bit of a reputation first. Then you take the plunge."

"You didn't. You left school when you were sixteen, worked in a canning factory for a few years, and saved up enough to buy a camera. Then you just took off for Vietnam and got famous."

Mr. Rent chuckles. "It wasn't that easy. And it was different then."

"Different how?"

"We were all nuts, for starters." He gets up to refill his glass with another generous amount of whisky. "But there were plenty of jobs to come back to in those days if you didn't make it. Not like now. And I got lucky with some of my early shots." He waves his arm, indicating the pictures on the walls. "Is that the kind of stuff you see yourself doing?"

"Sort of. Maybe more like looking at different ways people live and work, and what they have to do to survive."

"More of the social commentary. Less of the war stuff, eh?"

"Yeah. Like the ones you did of the child soldiers in Chad."

Mr. Rent mutters, "Jesus. That was a scene." He drains his glass and lies back in his chair, arms draped over the side. His eyes close.

Scab settles back too, listening to the strange music filling the apartment. He notices Mr.

Rent's glass about to slip from his hand, and jumps up to take it.

Mr. Rent opens his eyes and says, "Scab, my man," as if he's surprised to find him there. "Pour me another, will you?"

Scab refills the glass.

As he hands it back, Mr. Rent says, "It's not the best for relationships, you know, doing what we do."

Scab thinks of the picture of the beautiful Vietnamese girl.

"Just thought I'd mention it, in case you get yourself involved with that little Baptist University gal."

"I won't get involved with her," Scab scoffs.

Mr. Rent murmurs, "Right." His eyes slowly close again.

The talk of Philomena reminds Scab of his failure to tell her that he could have warned her about her attacker. He blurts out, "I shouldn't have taken that photograph."

Mr. Rent opens his eyes. "Meaning what?"

"She . . . the girl . . . she didn't know she was going to be on the front page."

"Doesn't matter. We don't need permission to take pictures that are in the public interest. Anyway, she'll love it. I've never met a woman yet that didn't like her fifteen minutes of fame." He leans back again, eyes closed.

"It's not just that. It's *how* I got the picture," Scab continues. "I could have warned her about the guy with the knife, but I didn't, because I was waiting . . . I *knew* there was going to be a good picture . . . If I hadn't waited . . ."

Mr. Rent snorts.

Scab glances at him. He leans forward to examine him more closely. Mr. Rent's head rolls back, his mouth open, empty glass resting on his stomach. Scab leans back and listens to the music, watching the cruise ship's slow progress towards its berth.

The music ends. Scab stands and looks down at Mr. Rent. He takes the glass and places it gently on the counter. Mr. Rent doesn't stir. Scab pads silently across the apartment and slips outside, closing the door quietly behind him, leaving Mr. Rent alone in his sparsely furnished apartment, with just the picture of the beautiful Vietnamese girl to keep him company.

HARBOURSIDE HIGH SCHOOL
SAINT JOHN
Co-operative Education Program
Final Report

Student: Julian Faye
Supervising teacher: Mr. Kinney
Placement: Saint John Chronicle (Photo Dept.)
Supervisor: Mr. Foster Rent, Chief Photographer

Workplace Skill Rating: 1-5
(5=exceptional, 1=needs improvement)
Comments:

Personal presentation & grooming . . . . ?
Grooming? Are we talking about a person or a dog?

Team player . . . . ?
What the hell's a team player?

Initiative 5
Plenty

Punctuality 5
Better than me, which can't be bad

Attitude 5
Lots

Any other comments: *Scab does great work. I'd give him a job on the Chronicle as a photo-journalist any day, except he's too good for it. I expect he'll get picked up by one of the big publications as soon as he's out of school.*

Signed: *Foster Rent, Chief Photographer, Saint John Chronicle*

THURSDAY, JULY 2ND

7:30 P.M.
FARM CRESCENT

Philomena is on the news again. Scab is on his way out to take pictures for his *Night in the City* series, but pauses when he hears her name. He peers into the living room, where his father is watching TV. It's the second time she's been on this week. The first was two days ago when she left the hospital. Now the reporter is saying she'll be the poster girl for the Outreach group.

The reporter goes on to say that the incident has brought in donations for the group. On TV, Philomena is smiling and shaking her head. She says that all the credit for the donations goes to the man who captured that image. Her rescuer, Julian Faye.

Scab wonders if his father will react to the mention of his name, but it doesn't seem to register.

His parents haven't spoken to him since graduation day. Scab, finally tiring of his mother's nagging, agreed at first to go to the ceremony, only to change his mind at the last minute, appalled at the thought of sitting among so many people. As the students lined up to march across the stage, he walked out, leaving his parents to look for him among the graduates, and during the announcement of the award for Outstanding Achievement in Art.

The interview ends, and the camera zooms in on Philomena. Scab stares at the screen, trying to see what the slash on her face looks like now. They said on the news a plastic surgeon had worked on it. He can't see much. The camera operator is sensitive enough not to linger too long on that side of her face. Scab picks at his own scar as he watches.

He walks quietly down the hall and out the door.

. . . .

8:05 P.M.
CITY HALL, DOWNTOWN
Two police, a man and a woman, approach Scab as he stands outside the Saint John Police Headquarters.

"Julian Faye?" the male officer inquires.

"How'd you know?"

They both grin and the female officer says, "The cameras are a bit of a giveaway."

Scab has the big Canon slung around his neck and the Olympus over his shoulder. He manages a grin.

The male officer says, "You're Mr. Rent's apprentice, and he wants you to spend a couple of hours on patrol, right?"

Scab nods.

"You'll stay in or beside the car at all times, and will not take any picture in which the subject can be identified. Okay?"

Scab nods again.

"You can call me Officer Brett and my colleague Officer Rachel, but we probably won't talk to you."

"Fine. Thanksh."

How could they know he's happiest when being ignored?

They have been patrolling the throughway for an hour when Officer Brett answers a radio call and says, "Domestic. Somerset."

Officer Rachel leaves the throughway at the next intersection, and within minutes they're at a duplex on Somerset. The police leave the car without speaking to Scab. As they enter the building, he gets out and leans on the roof of the car, watching the door they've gone through. Officer Rachel reappears, leading a woman to the patrol car, her arm around her. Then Officer Brett comes out, holding a man by the arm. The man suddenly shrugs him off, head-butts him, and throws himself at the woman with a roar. Officer Rachel turns to restrain him but the man knocks

99

her to the ground and lunges at the woman. He pins her against the cruiser and shakes her.

Scab, on the other side of the car, keeps shooting as the man draws his fist back. He takes one more frame, then lowers his camera and starts around the car, but has taken only two steps before the officers recover and are on the man. They throw him to the ground and Officer Brett kneels on his back while he handcuffs him.

They put the man in the back of the squad car, and while Officer Rachel leads the woman back inside, Officer Brett says, "I can't allow you to travel with us with this guy in the back. Sorry."

"Okay," Scab replies.

Officer Brett looks around. "It's not the best neighbourhood to leave you in."

"No problem."

"It'll be a problem for us if something happens to you. Why don't you get yourself up to Main before we leave here? That way I can watch until you get there and know you'll be okay."

"Sh-sure. Thanksh."

Scab has taken only a few steps when Officer Brett calls, "Hey. I thought you were going to grab that guy."

Scab hesitates, wondering what his answer should be. He mutters, "Thought about it."

Officer Brett shakes his head. "It's not your place to get involved. You're just the photographer. Got it?"

Scab nods, and walks on.

FRIDAY, JULY 3RD

6:45 P.M.
FARM CRESCENT

Scab is in his room, scrolling through the pictures he took the night of Philomena's injury. He knows he should delete the ones that prove he had plenty of time to warn her, but he can't bring himself to do it. Usually he ruthlessly trashes photographs he's not pleased with. But he is pleased with these; they're simply too good to delete.

Also, he likes zooming in on Philomena, and looking at the different ways the light catches her face.

He hears a knock at the front door, and his mother calls upstairs, "You have a visitor, Julian."

He wonders what kind of effort it must be for

her to speak to him. It's the first time since graduation. He doesn't answer. Maybe she'll think he's asleep and tell whoever it is to go away.

No chance.

"Julian! There's someone here to see you."

He shuts down the computer. He'll delete the pictures another time.

He goes slowly downstairs. Jordan is in the hallway.

"I knew you were up there," says Mrs. Faye. She looks at Jordan. "He gets so lost in his pictures sometimes that he's off in another world and doesn't hear anything."

Jordan sticks his hand out to shake Scab's. "Pastor Greg sent me. He was afraid you weren't getting his messages."

"What messages?" says Mrs. Faye. She looks at Scab.

He shrugs. "Dunno."

There had been three of them, once a week since the night of Philomena's injury, each one inviting Scab to join an Outreach meeting and urging him to visit Philomena again. She very much wanted to see her rescuer again, Pastor Greg had said. Scab was home each time the phone rang. As usual, he didn't answer. He later deleted the messages.

There had also been messages from radio and TV stations and newspapers, asking him to call. He'd ignored those, too. Scab's photograph of Philomena appeared in both the *Globe and Mail* and the *Toronto Star*. Both papers had picked up the story off the newswire. The story in the *Globe* referred to him as "the shy and reclusive photojournalist hero."

"Pastor Greg sent me to give you a ride to the meeting," Jordan says.

Scab starts, "I, er, I have to . . ."

"He said you wouldn't show up unless one of us came and got you — so here I am. I don't dare show up without you. Besides — it's a welcome back for Philomena."

Scab hesitates.

Jordan urges, "How about it?"

Scab shrugs. He can't see a way out.

* * *

"I'm sorry to arrive out of the blue like that," Jordan says, after a few minutes of driving in silence. "But you know what Pastor Greg's like. He said you'd have an excuse and not to take no for an answer. You know how he is about having things done the way he wants."

Like you didn't that night you left Philomena on her own.

Jordan seems to guess what Scab is thinking. "Thanks for not saying anything to him about me not staying with Philomena that night. I've apologized to her about it."

So we're both feeling guilty.

"I was going to say sorry to Pastor Greg, but

Philomena said not to, he didn't need to know, and you sort of implied I was there when you told him what happened . . ." Jordan takes his eyes off the road for a moment to glance at Scab. "So I owe you."

Scab shakes his head.

"I'm grateful. It must have been hard to lie . . ."

Hard for you, maybe. Seems to come easily enough to me.

"Philomena asks about you just about every time I see her, wanting to know if I've seen you or heard from you."

So Jordan's visited her lots of times. Probably every day. Scab thinks of the flowers beside the bed. *Jordan. XX.*

"She's worried that maybe she said something to offend you."

Scab shakes his head again.

"Ainsley and Brynn — Mr. and Mrs. Pippy — want to meet you, too."

Scab notes Jordan's casual use of first names. He's practically part of the family. It reminds Scab of his own status: not a member of the group.

Jordan chatters on. "Your photograph has brought in a ton of money. We were so short of funds a month ago Pastor Greg thought we'd have to give up the project. Everyone's really grateful. Now we may even have enough to expand the mission, thanks to you." Jordan describes the group's plans and their weekly meetings. When he stops at a red light, he glances at Scab again. "You don't say much, do you?"

Scab grunts.

"Don't worry about the meeting. Stick close to me. I'll get you through it."

Scab mumbles, "Thanksh."

. . . .

7:00 P.M.
BAPTIST UNIVERSITY

Jordan parks beside a No Parking sign.

When Jordan notices Scab looking at the sign, he grins. "It's Pastor Greg's car. He says most rules are designed to support the existence of the bureaucracy that enforces them and whose main aim is its own self-perpetuation."

Jordan leads the way to the room where Scab first met them a month before. As they arrive, two students are wheeling in a cart filled with refreshments.

Jordan stops. "I said the meeting was to welcome Philomena back. What I didn't tell you is that it's also to thank you for rescuing her and taking the photograph that's made our group . . . well, rich. So there are more people here than just us tonight. Parents, Philomena's friends and family, people from the university . . ."

Scab turns to leave.

Jordan grabs his sleeve. "Whoa. I knew you wouldn't come if I told you. But now you're here, you might as well stay. Please."

Scab pulls at his sleeve to free himself. He feels the familiar panic seizing him, taking over.

Jordan, looking at him, says, "Jesus, Scab. You look like shit. I didn't realize it was this bad for you. I could say you've got laryngitis and don't feel well, and you won't have to talk. Or I can do the talking for you. Or we can just sneak out . . ." He looks at Scab again. "Yeah. Let's sneak out."

Just then Pastor Greg appears at the classroom door. He strides forward, grabs Scab's hand, and pumps it up and down.

Jordan says quickly, "Julian's not well . . . He's got . . . laryngitis."

Pastor Greg says, "Poor Julian. You always seem to be in the wars for us." He puts his arm around Scab's shoulders and hustles him into the classroom. "Don't worry. Jordan can do the talking for you."

Jordan catches Scab's eye and shrugs.

Scab shrinks from the crowded room, but Pastor Greg's arm keeps him moving forward. He recognizes Mr. and Mrs. Pippy from the hospital, as well as some of the students who were on the mission. He can't see Philomena.

Pastor Greg booms, "Here he is — our saviour!"

Scab looks at the floor as everyone in the room applauds.

Pastor Greg goes on, "As most of you know, our Julian . . ."

"Our Julian"?

"Never says much . . ." He pauses to smile at Scab. "And we can expect even less from him tonight, as he has laryngitis and really shouldn't be here at all." He pauses again, this time for more applause to die down, before continuing, "However, I welcome him on behalf of the Outreach Mission, and invite him to attend our meetings. I also thank him again for so bravely and selflessly throwing himself between Philomena and her attacker, an act that not only saved her from even more serious injury, but also caused injury to himself. An injury that I see has still not entirely healed . . ."

Scab has made sure of that. It has become a habit to pick at it. Twice he's used scissors to start the bleeding again.

Pastor Greg waits for more applause to die down.

Scab looks up briefly. He thinks he sees Philomena's coffee-coloured hair at the back of the room.

". . . I also have to thank Julian for taking a photograph that captures both the reward and the danger our students experience on every mission. A photograph that, through the interest and concern it has generated, has brought us more funding than we have ever had before." He pauses for another round of applause before going on, "As you know, we're also here this evening to welcome our own Philomena back with us tonight."

Everyone claps again. The crowd starts to close in around Scab at the front of the room and

Philomena at the back. Scab loses sight of her hair as people press around him, wanting to shake his hand and echo Pastor Greg's praise. Scab keeps his head down, occasionally nodding in response. He glances up twice, just long enough to scan the room for Philomena. He feels a hand press softly on his arm. He turns to find Mrs. Pippy beside him. She leads him a few feet away from the crowd.

"You darling boy," she says.

Darling?

"How can I ever thank you for saving our dear Philomena?"

You mean for letting her get scarred for life.

Scab's head drops further.

Mrs. Pippy squeezes his arm. "You don't have to say anything. I know you're not well, and that you don't like to talk, anyway. Philomena told us all about you. But I have to let you know that what you did was noble and selfless. And at the same time, you captured a very moving image in an important moment of Philomena's life." She adds, "We do wish you'd visited her again. She so much wanted you to . . ."

"Sh-sorry."

"Please don't apologize. We understand . . ."

You don't.

" . . . how hard you find situations — social situations. I'll let Brynn talk about your photograph, and about how we plan to express our gratitude and admiration for it."

Scab, his head still down, hasn't noticed Mr. Pippy approach. He shakes Scab's hand and bends to murmur in his ear, "You want to get the hell out of here — right?"

Scab looks up.

"Of course right," Mr. Pippy continues. "I don't blame you. So do I. I'll be in touch about your picture."

He shakes Scab's hand again, and Mrs. Pippy hugs him with an apologetic, "May I?"

As they move away, Jordan takes their place beside Scab. "How're you holding up?"

"Okay. Thanksh."

"Philomena wants to talk to you. She's been doing the celebrity thing ever since she got here, like you, and couldn't get clear. But here she is now."

He steps away.

Scab fixes his eyes on the floor. He can't look up. He feels, rather than sees, the people around him fall back, leaving him in an island of space.

He feels exposed. Vulnerable.

It feels as if he's in a dream where he's naked in the street. He sees space on the floor around him. He feels the urge to escape, but he can't move. His eyes are still on the floor, and now he sees her feet moving towards him. He remembers her sneakers with green laces from the night of the mission. The hem of her short navy dress comes into view. He doesn't want it to seem as if he's looking at her legs, so he raises his eyes, past the dress, past the jacket with the flowers on the sleeves. He finds himself blushing, as if he's been appraising her.

His eyes reach her face. He hopes they don't show his shock over the zipper-like scar that razes across her cheek. The skin around it is puckered and white against the rose that is the rest of her face. The scar pulls one side of her mouth up, distorting it into a parody of a permanent smile

I could have saved you from this.

His fingers twitch, wanting to get at his own, insignificant, scar.

"May I?" she asks, echoing her mother as she holds her arms towards him. She hugs him and the onlookers applaud.

She has the same lemony scent he remembers from sitting close beside her in the van. He is aware of her body pressing against his. He thinks of Jordan ripping open her dress in the alley and that glimpse of her bra. She kisses him on the cheek, on his scar.

He wishes she'd sink her teeth into it, rip it open.

Jordan steps forward. "Don't the rest of you have anything to talk about?"

The onlookers laugh and resume their conversations. Jordan retreats, leaving Scab and Philomena.

She whispers, "You don't have laryngitis, do you?"

He hangs his head.

"I won't tell. Why didn't you come and see me again?"

"I don't belong."

And I'm too ashamed.

"Of course you belonged there, with me. Like you belong here, with our group. I'd like you to be here for every meeting." She grins. "As far as Pastor Greg is concerned you're already one of us. He'll probably send someone to pick you up every time." She adds, "Will you come next week?"

Jordan, who has been hovering nearby, moves closer. "Sorry to interrupt, but you know what's coming up next. It's about time for the fellowship circle."

Pastor Greg is already at the front of the room, holding his hands up for silence.

Jordan mutters, "Do you want to stay for it?"

"No."

As they slip out of the classroom, they hear Pastor Greg's voice boom from behind them, "Let us form our circle of fellowship."

"Will he mind?" says Scab.

"He'll be too wrapped up in his praying to notice," says Jordan. "Anyway, he told me to run you home."

* * *

Jordan and Philomena sit in the front seats of Pastor Greg's car. Scab wonders if they'll stop to make out on their way back to the mission. He sees Philomena's reflection in the rear-view mirror. She's smiling, the scar lifting her mouth higher on one side than the other, so that now it's more leering scowl than distorted smile.

In the darkness of the back seat, he fingers his own scar, scratching at it until he feels his fingers sticky with blood.

FRIDAY, JULY 17TH

5:45 P.M.
FARM CRESCENT
Scab pores over the photographs he took on the night of Philomena's injury, steeling himself to delete them once and for all.

There's an hour before Jordan is due to pick him up. Scab can't decide which is worse: To attend the meeting and have to make conversation and endure the physical contact of the fellowship circle that he's sure he won't be able to avoid again. Or not to attend, and feel a letdown he can't understand.

His mother calls to him, but he doesn't answer. He stares at the sequence of pictures leading up to the attack.

His mother calls again.

He can't decide where to start deleting. He works backwards from the photo that was used in the newspapers. The one before it is only slightly different — the stalker a quarter-step back, Philomena's head at a slightly different angle, the two details making the composition of the photo unbalanced, less pleasing. He zooms in on Philomena. He's caught her face in perfect profile in this one. He scrolls through several more frames until he comes to one of Jordan scuffling with Charlie. This is where he should start deleting. He works his way back through the photographs. Surely he could keep just one or two of the frames preceding the attack. He may use them — one day, when everything has blown over — in a lecture on capturing the perfect moment, like Mr. Rent does when he lectures to camera clubs.

"That isn't the picture that's getting all the attention, is it?" he hears behind him.

His mother is looking over his shoulder. He's been so absorbed in the photos he didn't hear her come upstairs.

"Er . . . no."

He closes the window quickly.

"It looked just like it, except the man was further back."

She's more observant than I thought.

"When did you first see him?"

"Who?"

"The man, of course."

"Just as I took that picture."

"But then you wouldn't have taken the one that's getting all the attention, where he's closer to the girl . . ." She looks at him strangely. "Not unless you kept taking pictures while you watched him get closer."

He mutters, "I don't know. Everything happened so fast."

She says, "Hmmm." Her voice turns coy and teasing. "Well, she's here now."

"Who?"

"The one in the picture. I've been calling you, but you ignore me, as usual. She says she's here to see you."

He follows his mother downstairs. Philomena is in the hallway.

"I told you, dear — he was busy with his pictures," Mrs. Faye says. "A bomb could go off while he's up there and he wouldn't notice."

Philomena grins at Scab. "I've come to get you."

"I was expecting Jordan."

"He's under threat from Pastor Greg to finish a report."

Scab follows her outside, to a Lexus parked at the end of the drive.

Philomena explains, "Mom let me have her car."

"You're early."

"Do you mind?"

"'Course not."

She turns right at the end of Farm Crescent, away from the downtown and the Baptist University.

"Where are we going?"

"Have I got you worried?" She glances at him, grinning. "Are you afraid I'm abducting you?"

"'Course not."

She looks at him again, still grinning. "You never know your luck." She pauses to make a left turn before going on, "Actually, I'm early because we have an appointment before we go to the Outreach meeting. I mean — you have an appointment — with my dad, at his gallery."

"His *gallery?*"

"He's part owner of an art gallery. Didn't he tell you?"

"Your mom jusht shaid he had a plan, shomething to do with the photograph and shaying thank you, and then he shaid he'd be in touch."

"Well this is him getting in touch — through me. I told him there was no point in phoning you, because you never answered the phone and you ignored messages." She sneaks another glance at him. "Right?"

"I guessh."

She shakes her head. "You're a strange one, Scab."

Now he knows where they are heading. The Gallery District is in the old part of the city.

During the past two years, a cluster of galleries, arts and crafts stores, and cafés has sprung up there.

Philomena drives through a maze of narrow streets and pulls up at what looks from the outside like an old-fashioned, glass-fronted store. Above the door, and across the top of the windows on each side of it, sit the words, *Images and Expressions*.

. . . .

6:15 P.M.
GALLERY DISTRICT

Philomena pauses at the door. "You'll be all right, won't you, talking to my father?"

Scab says, "Sure." He's suddenly aware that he seems to have his lisp under control.

The gallery is brightly lit. There's no furniture except a few benches in the middle of the long, narrow space. Abstract paintings, with wild colours and jagged shapes, hang on the walls. Three visitors contemplate them. Scab has read about the gallery in the *Chronicle*. According to the paper's art critic, Images and Expressions stages "Saint John's most challenging and exciting exhibitions."

Mr. Pippy and a woman in a business suit, who doesn't look much older than Philomena, are sitting on stools at the end of the gallery. Mr. Pippy strides forward, hugs Philomena, and shakes hands with Scab. "Thank you for coming. This is Marilyn Lescott, co-owner of the gallery."

The woman also shakes his hand. "I'm an admirer of your work, not just the photograph that's currently making you famous, but others I've seen in the *Chronicle*. We'd like to help your career. I'll let Brynn tell you about that."

Mr. Pippy takes Scab's arm. "Let me tell you what I have in mind." He steers Scab towards the stools, while Marilyn and Philomena start a tour of the gallery. Mr. Pippy goes on, "Every year, Images and Expressions features the work of two or three emerging artists. Marilyn and I would like you to be one of them. A selection of your photographs will hang here for a month, the three of us deciding together which ones to use from your collection. The show will give your work even more exposure than it's getting now, and you'd probably even sell a few prints. Consider this a 'thank you' from Philomena's mother and me for all that you've done for her. But also, Marilyn and I believe your work merits it, and part of what Images and Expressions does is promote the work of promising young artists."

"Thank you."

"We have an opening in August. The artist whose work we booked for that time seems to have fled the city — leaving behind a lot of debts, it looks like. We'll need something like a couple of dozen prints. Why don't you make a preliminary selection of, say, forty pictures by the end of this week? Then you and I and Marilyn will get together as soon as we can after that and narrow it down to the show prints. That should give us just enough time to get the photos to our Toronto lab for printing and mounting and framing, and for the lab to ship them back to us. Then we can decide together how best to hang them. Images and Expressions will pay for all of this, and gets twenty percent of anything you sell. Agreed?"

"Of course. Thank you," Scab says, stunned.

"On another matter . . ." Mr. Pippy lowers his voice as he glances across to where Philomena and Marilyn Lescott are engrossed in conversation. "Philomena's injuries . . ."

Are my fault.

"Are not all on the outside. The scar on her stomach is superficial and once healed will only be visible if she insists on wearing one of her ridiculously small bikinis on the beach."

Scab thrusts away the mental image of Philomena in a bikini.

"But the scar on her face, while it will become less noticeable, will be there for the rest of her life. She's going to counselling to help her deal with it, but she still thinks the scar makes her hideous and will alienate people — I mean boyfriends, men — from her for the rest of her life. Now, Philomena thinks a lot of you . . ."

Only because she doesn't know what I did. What I failed to do.

". . . and Ainsley and I would appreciate all the help and support you can give her to help her deal with the injury."

119

Haven't I done enough already?

"I'll try."

"I know you will."

* * *

As Scab and Philomena leave the gallery, Philomena suddenly says, "Let's get a coffee and skip the meeting."

"Will Pastor Greg mind?"

"He might, but it's the last meeting of the year, and he'll have forgotten by next September."

She leads the way across the street to a small café, where they sit in a corner by the window.

Scab asks, "What about Jordan?"

"What about him?"

"He'll be expecting to see you, won't he?"

"Term's finished. He hung around to finish some work, but now he's leaving. He lives on the north shore and has a summer job up there."

"Will you see him during the break?"

"I doubt it. He can't get time off, and Dad's got a job for me at the gallery, so I won't have time to travel." She grins at Scab. "Are you surprised?"

"I thought he was your boyfriend."

"He thought he was, too, until yesterday. I told him he was a good friend, and always would be, but no more than that."

SATURDAY, JULY 18TH

7:00 P.M.
FARM CRESCENT
Scab is working on his *Night in the City* photographs. Mr. Rent has promised to run them in a series in the *Chronicle*, starting the next week. Scab closes the *Night* pictures and opens the file he's labelled P, for Philomena. He's scrolling through the shots leading up to the attack, trying, again, to delete them, when the telephone rings downstairs, and his mother calls out, "Julian, it's for you."

"It's me. What are you doing?"

Philomena.

"Working on photographs. What are you doing?"

"I'm on duty at the gallery and I found a note

from Dad asking me to call and make sure you're still coming on Monday. You have to help make the final selection of photos."

"'Course."

"I knew you'd remember, but I thought I'd call, anyway. What photos are you working on?"

"*Night in the City.* Mr. Rent's going to start running them next week. There's only one more shoot — the old hot-dog stand on King Street — and I'll do that tomorrow night."

He can't think of anything else to say. Philomena is silent, too. Scab is aware of his mother listening to him from the kitchen.

Eventually Philomena says, "I guess I should get back to work. I'll see you at the gallery."

"Are you working Monday?"

"Not until the afternoon. I've got some errands to do downtown in the morning. I have to see my therapist again." Philomena sighs. "Today she told me I'll always have image issues, and I have to learn to deal with them."

Image issues. Like a lisp. Like a scar.

"Hey," she adds suddenly, brightly, "why don't we meet downtown on the boardwalk, around noon, when I've finished the stuff I have to do? We can walk to the gallery together."

After the call, Scab returns to his pictures of Philomena on the night of the attack. He pores over them, trying to decide where to start deleting. He zooms in on a shot of Philomena and gazes at her face — the ochre eyes, the turned-up nose, the narrow lips, the pocked skin smoothed by the dim light. He interposes the scar that turns her smile into a sneer.

"I'll always have image issues, and I have to learn to deal with them."

He stands abruptly and moves to the mirror in his room and pictures it — not the insignificant scratch he got that night, but a real scar — on his own face.

You're morose and ugly, but at least you're not disfigured for life. Why didn't you get scarred, instead of her? You've got nothing to lose, he tells his reflection.

Scab fingers the little wound. It's dry, and he can feel a crust of new skin forming over it. He picks at it again until it flakes away. It lies on the floor, like the wing of an insect.

He returns his gaze to the mirror. Now the cut is a puckered, white-edged scar. He digs his fingernails into it. It turns a blotchy red, but it holds up. He tries again, digging harder, with the same result, leaving an indent that slowly fills. He finds the little pocket knife he keeps in his camera bag for emergency repairs and examines his face in the mirror again.

This is what you deserve for being a cold, lying coward, who cares more about his precious photographs than about someone's safety, he snarls silently.

He carefully inserts the tip of the blade in the scar and presses.

Nothing happens.

He digs deeper.

Still nothing.

He shifts his grip on the knife and holds it horizontally, the tip of the cutting edge of the blade at the end of the scar. He applies gentle pressure.

No give. No pain. No blood.

He takes a deep breath and digs the blade fiercely into his skin, at the same time slicing the length of the wound and beyond.

He holds the knife away from his face, while he waits for the blood and the pain.

Finally, two drops of blood appear, and a third, joining into a stream as they trickle down his cheek.

And at last it hurts.

SUNDAY, JULY 19TH

10:50 P.M.
KING STREET

Scab has been standing in the unlit doorway of an out-of-business pub for four hours, alternately squatting on his haunches and leaning against the door. The entrance is littered with empty chip bags, cigarette butts, and takeout-coffee cups. He is watching and shooting the hot-dog stand across the street.

Earlier in the evening, he captured parents buying treats for their kids after walking on the harbourside trail and tired shoppers snacking as they trailed from Brunswick Square. Now it's drinkers spilling from the bars in search of cheap eats. There's a small crowd of them around the stand.

Through their shouts and laughter, Scab hears, "You must halt whenever you approach a stopped school bus with its upper alternating red lights flashing, regardless of whether you are behind the bus or approaching it from the front."

Scab hasn't seen or heard Road Safety Charlie since the night of the attack. Charlie lurches down King Street and approaches the stand. The crowd parts for him. The stand operator waves at him to move on. Scab raises his camera.

Charlie shouts, "When approaching the bus from the front, stop at a safe distance for children to get off the bus and cross the road in front of you."

The people in the street cheer, and someone shouts, "You tell him, Charlie."

Two men who have been standing in the darkness beside the entrance to Brunswick Square move quickly forward, grasp Charlie by each arm, and hustle him down King Street, away from the stand. They release him with a shove that sends him staggering further down the street.

He turns and roars, "If you are coming from behind the bus, stop at least twenty metres away. Do not go until the bus moves or the lights have stopped flashing."

The crowd cheers again. The two men run at him and he flees. They return to the stand, laughing. They take chips and pop from the stand and return to the shadows. The crowd moves away, some glancing nervously back at the men.

Scab takes a break from shooting to look through the sequence of pictures he has just captured. He cocks his head at the sound of weeping. The Crying Man has been wailing somewhere nearby all evening.

Scab wonders how he can still be on the street. If the police had recognized him as the man in the image, they'd either not bothered with an arrest, or they'd taken him in and he'd already been in — and out of — court.

The sound of crying gets closer.

Scab peers from his doorway. At the same time a car pulls up in front of his hideout. Philomena climbs out, holding a thermos and two cups.

Scab says, "Wha—"

She runs to his doorway, smiling her twisted smile. "I came to visit."

She kicks aside a couple of Styrofoam cups and they sit, huddled close together, among the chip bags and cigarette butts. She pours coffee.

Scab says, "What are you doing here?"

"I told you — visiting, and bringing you refreshments when you're working. You said you'd be here tonight, taking pictures." She pulls a sandwich bag from her pocket and offers Scab a buttered muffin. "Actually I'm on my way to pick up my folks from a dinner party. They didn't want to have to drive home, and I said I'd get them so they didn't have to bother with a taxi." She looks right at Scab. "Sad, isn't it — an eighteen-year-old girl with nothing to do tonight except look after

127

her parents? You'd think she'd have something better to do."

Scab looks down.

The Crying Man's weeping is closer.

Why can't Philomena hear it, too?

"This is fun," Philomena says. She peers out from the doorway. There's a lull in the street activity. The hot-dog stand is now empty except for the operator, who is cleaning his equipment, and the men in the shadows behind him.

"It's like a romance movie! A boy and a girl sitting on the sidewalk at night in a dirty doorway. What d'you suppose would happen next — if we were in a movie?" She looks directly at him again.

Scab struggles for something to say. He wishes he could do small talk.

He drains his coffee and mutters, "Thanks."

"Am I being dismissed?"

He says quickly, "'Course not. Sh-sorry."

She leans against him briefly in a little nudge. "Relax. I'm *joking*."

"I know."

They sit in silence.

The sound of weeping starts again, even closer.

Philomena says, "Someone's crying."

The Crying Man appears on the opposite sidewalk. He stops and sits on the edge of a raised flower bed, his face in his hands.

"What's wrong with him?"

"Don't know. He's always been like that."

"Poor man."

Poor man nothing. He slashed you for the sake of a necklace.

The Crying Man lifts his head from his hands to draw a breath before releasing another series of wails.

Philomena is staring. "It's him, isn't it?" she says slowly, her hand drifting to the scar on her face.

Scab nods. He feels a surge of anger towards the Crying Man. What does he have to cry about? He isn't scarred and disfigured for life.

Philomena looks away, from the Crying Man and Scab. Her hand still covers the scar. Scab thinks she is crying. He knows he should comfort her.

What would Jordan do, with his easy, commanding confidence?

"I guess I should go," Philomena says.

No. Please stay.

The Crying Man has stopped crying. He's staring at the hot-dog stand, where the operator is hanging a spatula from a hook at the side of the cart. It swings there, gleaming, the street lights shining on it.

Philomena moves to stand. Scab hauls himself to his feet quickly and offers his hand to help her up. She takes it, smiling lopsidedly. Her hand is smooth and cold. He wishes he had the courage to hold on to it.

Don't go.

They gather the thermos and cups.

The Crying Man is moving slowly towards the stand, his eyes fixed now on the gleaming spatula. The operator eyes him.

Scab walks with Philomena to the car. He carries the thermos in one hand and his camera in the other.

The Crying Man has stopped. The street is quiet, and Scab hears the operator say, "What do you want?" The men behind the stand stir.

Philomena pauses beside the door of the car, looking at Scab.

If we were friends — like, boyfriend and girlfriend — is this when we'd hug, kiss goodbye?

He doesn't move, and she climbs into the car.

Scab says, "Thanks for the coffee and sh-stuff."

Her eyes flicker from Scab to the Crying Man and back to Scab.

Are you trying to tell me something?

The Crying Man takes half a step towards the hot-dog stand and freezes again. Scab shifts his grip on the camera, feeling the shutter release under his index finger.

Philomena looks up at him. "Will you be all right?"

"What d'you mean?"

"Don't you have to be careful, downtown at night, alone?"

"I'm good at not being noticed."

She smiles jaggedly. "Well — see you."

He nods.

Is that the best you can do — a nod?

130

She pulls away.

Scab watches her go, then retreats to his doorway and sights the camera on the Crying Man, who takes another half-step towards the stand.

The operator says, "Get out of here, weirdo."

The two men emerge from the shadows. The Crying Man leaps at the stand, grabs the spatula, and takes off with it. The men from the shadows lumber after him. The Crying Man bolts across the street and runs towards Scab's hiding place. The men are close behind.

Scab is frozen in his doorway, holding the camera behind him. As they run past, he glimpses the Crying Man's knife in his hand.

Scab waits.

He peers from his hiding place. A taxi cruises past. The hot-dog stand operator has resumed cleaning his grill. No one else is in sight. Scab takes a last photograph of the stand, the tired operator cleaning up, zooming out to show the empty space around him, to emphasize his lonely occupation.

He tucks his camera into his jacket and saunters down the sidewalk in the same direction that the Crying Man took. He hears low voices, a thud, a burst of laughter, from a side street ahead of him. Then the men from the stand emerge. Scab feels their eyes on him. He keeps his head down until they pass.

He turns into the street they came out of. He

looks back over his shoulder a few seconds later. They are gone.

There is no sign of the Crying Man.

Scab walks slowly on, looking left and right. He comes to a narrow alley with a light at each end, darkness between.

A soft whimpering drifts from the gloom.

Scab makes out a shape halfway along the alley. The whimpers become sobs. Scab approaches cautiously and looks down. The Crying Man lies on his back, his legs bent under him, his arms flung wide. Blood is trickling from his nose and mouth, and two wine-red bruises mark his cheek. His knife lies beside him and a slash across his forehead leaks blood that mixes with the familiar tears pouring down his cheeks.

Scab moves to allow the sparse light to fall on the Crying Man's face. He photographs the hopeless, crumpled shape in the dark alley, then leans over him to photograph his battered, bloody face. For a moment, through the viewfinder, he sees Philomena's distorted smile. He thinks of how different she is from him. Neither of them wanted to turn the Crying Man in. But for different reasons. Scab because he does not — can not — make himself feel. Philomena because she cares too much. She and her friends at the Baptist Outreach. Finally, Scab feels something. Rage.

He picks up the knife and, holding the camera to one side, leans over the Crying Man again. Pressing the tip of the blade against his bloodied cheek, he murmurs, "How does it feel when you're the one getting slashed? How about I give you a scar like hers?"

But instead, Scab straightens up slowly, throws the knife away, and walks back up the alley. On King Street, the hot-dog stand has gone, and the men with it. Scab heads for the bus stop. When he passes one of the few remaining public phones, he hesitates, then calls 9-1-1.

"There's a man in Jardine's Alley, beaten up," he says, then puts the phone down quickly. He walks on, hesitates again, and turns back.

* * *

In the alley the Crying Man is half-sitting, slumped against the wall, sobbing. Blood and tears mix as they run down his face. Scab pulls a lens-cleaning tissue from his pocket and offers it to him, muttering, "It's all I've got.".

The Crying Man takes it, eyeing Scab suspiciously.

"You'll be all right," Scab says as he crouches beside him. He stays until the police car and ambulance pull up at the end of the alley, then he scuttles to the other end and runs for the bus.

MONDAY, JULY 20TH

12:00 P.M.
THE BOARDWALK, DOWNTOWN

Scab sees Philomena before she sees him. She's
looking across the harbour as she strolls towards
him on the harbourside trail. She's wearing a long
sundress that the breeze swirls around her ankles.
He photographs her just before she turns and sees
him. He wonders whether Mr. Rent is sitting at his
big picture window now, watching.

How would his meeting with Philomena appear
to his mentor?

Philomena waves, and Scab lifts his hand in
acknowledgement. Her hair looks different, and as
she gets nearer, he sees that, instead of the
ponytail, it's styled so that it curls forward on each

side of her face, partly covering the scar. Scab isn't sure whether it hides it, or just draws more attention to it. He wonders whether he should comment, afraid that anything he says will come out wrong.

"I like your hair."

"I don't. But my therapist told Mom I should try it."

They set off for the gallery district. On the way they pass a playground, derelict and deserted. Scab stops to take a picture. Then stops, remembering what Mr. Rent once told him: "You don't take pictures. You *make* them." What could he do to make the playground a better picture?

Philomena says, "What are you thinking?"

"Will you dance in that playground for a photograph?" he asks her.

She rolls her eyes. "Okay. But only with a disguise."

They find a used-clothing store nearby and dig through the bins until Philomena finds a flowered hat with a wide brim, a shawl, and a Panama hat.

Scab asks, "Why d'you need two hats?"

Philomena grins. "You'll see."

They return to the playground, and Philomena improvises a dance — pirouetting, skipping, swooping up and down. Scab photographs her with the dilapidated slide and climbing frames and swings in the background, one side of a swing dangling, unhooked from its rusty chain.

Philomena stops.

Scab says, "One more."

"Only if you dance with me."

"No."

"No photograph, then."

"But I have to take the picture."

"You can set the camera on the timer, can't you?"

He hesitates.

Philomena stands close to him with her hand on his arm. "*Please,* Scab."

He balances the camera on the backrest of a broken-down bench at the side of the playground and sets the timer for twenty seconds. He stands facing Philomena, his hands at his sides, while the camera beeps its way to firing the shutter. "What am I supposed to do?"

She produces the Panama hat from behind her and places it on his head. Then she moves close to him and takes his hands. He tries to pull them away, but she holds on. She places one of his hands on her shoulder and the other around her waist, and puts her arms around him.

"What are you doing?"

"Getting us ready to do a slow dance, dummy."

Scab glances around him. He's relieved to see there's no one in sight. They shuffle through the weeds of the gravel bed, Philomena leading. Just before the shutter fires, she rests her head on his shoulder.

. . . .

GALLERY DISTRICT

When they reach the gallery, Scab and Philomena find the forty pictures Scab has chosen laid out on a trestle table in the middle of the room. Mr. Pippy and Marilyn Lescott are going through them. Mr. Pippy has reading glasses perched on the end of his nose. Scab joins them, while Philomena goes into the office.

"We have to reduce your selection to twenty-four," says Mr. Pippy. "Are there any that you absolutely want in the show?"

Scab points out the man and child at the window during the hotel fire, the man in the domestic dispute with his fist drawn back, the woman in the alley giving the world the finger, Jordan tussling with Road Safety Charlie, and the shot of the Crying Man stalking Philomena.

As he points out the last picture, he glances through the open door of the office, where Philomena is working at the computer, and mumbles, "Don't want to upset Philomena, though . . ."

"She's used to seeing it," says Mr. Pippy.

Marilyn Lescott chooses a set, including the shoppers in the city market, the teens on a carnival ride at night, and the three-legged dog in a shop doorway. Then Mr. Pippy makes his choice, including the Crying Man and the startled tourists, and a portrait of Mr. and Mrs. Faye sitting on a beach, looking in opposite directions.

"Will your parents mind if we use this?" he asks Scab.

Scab shrugs.

Marilyn Lescott counts the pictures they've chosen. "Twenty-four. Are you happy with the selection, Julian?"

He nods.

Mr. Pippy calls, "We're ready, Phil."

Philomena appears from the office, carrying a tray set out with glasses. Mr. Pippy produces a bottle of champagne.

"We always celebrate the final selection," he explains. "It's a tradition at the gallery."

Mr. Pippy passes them all a glass and says, "Congratulations to the artist on his first exhibition."

He raises his glass towards Scab. Philomena and Marilyn Lescott do the same.

"Maybe no one will come," Scab says.

"They'll come," says Marilyn Lescott.

"Or the people who do come will think the pictures stink," Scab worries.

Philomena rolls her eyes. "Listen to him."

"We have a big mailing list," says Mr. Pippy. "There'll be a crowd for the opening, and some of them will want to talk to you, Julian. Can you handle that?"

Scab nods.

Philomena grins. "First we dance in the street, and now you say you'll talk to people. You're cutting loose, aren't you?"

Marilyn Lescott laughs. "Where were you dancing?"

"In an old playground. Show them the pictures, Scab."

He finds the pictures on his camera and holds the monitor towards Mr. Pippy and Marilyn Lescott. Mr. Pippy takes the camera from Scab and holds it so that everyone can look more closely.

"I like these," Marilyn Lescott mutters as they scroll through them. "Especially this one — two clowns celebrating life in the rubble!" She holds the camera for Scab to see. It's the last frame, the photo of Scab and Philomena, in their hats, slow dancing. "I want to include it in the show." She glances at Mr. Pippy, who nods. "Can we use it, Julian?"

"I'd need to work on it at home first," Scab says cautiously.

"We need it — like — two hours ago," Marilyn Lescott warns.

"Do it right now," says Mr. Pippy. "Philomena can take my car and drive you home, and wait while you do the work. Then bring it straight back here. We need to get all the pictures off to the lab right away if they're going to be ready for the opening."

. . . .

3:45 P.M.
FARM CRESCENT

Getting out of the car at Farm Crescent, Scab says, "This won't take me long. Do you want to come in, or wait in the car?"

Philomena laughs. "I'll come in, of course. Unless you don't want me to."

"My parents are weird."

"Everyone's parents are weird."

"Mom will be all over you. You'd better come up to my room . . ." Scab finds himself blushing, as if he's propositioning her in some way. "If that's okay with you. Otherwise she'll interrogate you non-stop."

"Didn't you say you had lots of photos hanging in your room? I'll look at them while you work."

Mrs. Faye appears as soon as Scab opens the door. "Philomena's going to wait while I get another picture ready for the show," he says.

Mrs. Faye says, "It's nice to see you again. We're so happy Julian has a nice friend like you. He's so shy and sensitive, he finds it difficult to make friends . . ."

Thanks, Ma. That'll help.

"Gorman, come out here and say hello to Julian's friend. Can I get you anything, dear? A cup of tea, orange juice, milk, a cookie?"

Philomena smiles and says, "No thank you."

Scab manages to interrupt, "I have to work on the picture. It's urgent."

He sets off up the stairs, Philomena following.

His mother starts up the stairs behind them until Mr. Faye, who has joined them in the hallway, says, "Give the kids a minute's peace for Christ's sake."

Mrs. Faye calls after Scab, "The phone's been ringing for you, Mr. Rent and another gentleman. They both said they'd call back. Mr. Rent's called three times."

"Okay," Scab says.

In his room, Philomena looks at the photos he has pinned on the walls, including a set he took of his parents, his mother looking as if she is worrying about something, his father stern and forbidding. In one picture, his father stares straight at the camera, while his mother looks into the distance, wistfully.

"It's like she's searching for something," Philomena says.

"Yeah — her life," snorts Scab. "She's wondering how she's ended up living here with someone who hardly talks to her."

Then Philomena watches over his shoulder as he downloads the pictures of their dance in the playground.

The telephone rings.

"It's the gentleman who called earlier," Scab's mom calls up to him.

Scab tells Philomena, "I'd better go see. I'll be back in a sec."

He goes downstairs and takes the phone. "Hello?"

"Mr. Julian Faye? This is Mike Hamm, from the Professional Photographers' Association. Congratulations. You've just been named Young Photographer of the Year for your picture of the young woman being stalked while doing charity work. The award will be announced in the morning. The decision was unanimous. The award committee agreed they'd seen few images so well composed and executed under difficult conditions, no matter the age of the photographer."

"Thank you."

"You can expect a lot of media and professional attention from this. Do you have someone who can help you out?"

"Foster Rent."

"Of course. You'll receive an invitation to attend the convention in Toronto next month as a special guest, with your family, of course. The award will be presented then. I'll hope to see you there."

As soon as Scab hangs up, the phone rings again. He stares at it.

His mother appears from the living room. "Aren't you going to answer it? It'll be Mr. Rent again."

His father shouts, "Answer the damn thing!"

Scab picks up the phone. "Hello?"

"Good grief. Are you all right?" Mr. Rent says.

"Why?"

"You answered the phone. It's the first time I've known that to happen."

"What's up?"

"Have you heard?"

"I just got a call from Mr. Hamm."

"I heard a few hours ago from an old friend on the awards committee. I've been trying to reach you."

"I was getting ready for the show."

"Have you decided what camera you're going to get?"

"What do you mean?"

"The award comes with a new camera of your choice."

Scab murmurs, "No shit," and falls silent.

After a few seconds, Mr. Rent says, "Are you still there? You're quite the celebrity, aren't you — first your own show, then Young Photographer of the Year. Congratulations."

Scab senses Mr. Rent about to hang up and says, "Hey."

"What?"

"Thanks for nominating me, and for . . . you know."

Mr. Rent says, "Forget it," and hangs up.

Mrs. Faye is still hovering beside Scab. She says, "What was all that about?"

"I'll tell you later."

He wants Philomena to be the first to know.

He sets off up the stairs.

Stops.

Shit.

He has left her in his room with the computer on.

After two minutes of idleness, the monitor goes to screensaver.

He has been on the phone to Mr. Hamm for five minutes, and to Mr. Rent for another three.

The screensaver is set to show Scab's pictures file, changing screens at three-second intervals.

He runs up the remaining stairs.

He freezes in his doorway.

Philomena is staring at the screen.

The pictures passing across it are those leading up to her attack, showing her assailant moving stealthily forward, like a frame-by-frame movie of the night of the attack.

She turns around slowly.

She stares at Scab.

TUESDAY, JULY 21ST

1:30 A.M.
WATER STREET

It's well after midnight when Scab knocks softly at Mr. Rent's apartment door. After a few seconds, he hears the shuffle of feet.

Mr. Rent opens the door a crack, sees Scab, then swings it wide. "Jesus Christ, Scab."

Scab puts his hand to his cheek. He feels, with satisfaction, the two sides of the wound hanging open, like lips pouting. The blood has started to coagulate, but is still trickling from the wound. His chin is sticky with it, and the front of his shirt is wet with it.

Mr. Rent repeats, "Jesus Christ, Scab. Have you been in a fight, or what?"

"She found out."

"Found out what?"

"That I kept shooting when I could have warned her."

"And she attacked you?"

"No. I did this-sh."

"You need stitches."

Scab shakes his head.

Mr. Rent puts down the drink he is holding and takes Scab by the hand, like a child. He leads him inside and guides him to a chair. The music they listened to on Scab's last visit is playing softly.

Mr. Rent disappears into the bathroom and returns with a bottle and a wad of gauze and a roll of tape. He dabs rubbing alcohol on the cut, pulls the sides together, and places the gauze gently over it, smoothing it down tenderly, all the time muttering, "Jesus Christ, Scab," and shaking his head. When he's dressed the wound, he says, "Come over here in the light so I can see if it's going to hold."

Scab stands under the light in the kitchenette while Mr. Rent peers closely at his work. He nods. "That'll do, but I still think you need to go to emergency."

Scab shakes his head again.

"You won't make a habit of cutting yourself like this, will you?"

When Scab doesn't answer, Mr. Rent grabs him by the shoulders and shakes him. "Will you?"

He suddenly pulls Scab to him, embracing him,

and mutters, "Scab, my man, I'm sorry."

He releases him and inspects the dressing again. Satisfied, he pours Scab a glass of brandy and says, "You better get this down yourself."

They sit in the chairs in front of the picture window.

Mr. Rent asks, "How did she find out?"

"She came to the houshe. We were looking at picturesh on the computer when you and Mr. Hamm called. I left her in my room and the shcreenshaver came up with my photosh."

"What did she say?"

"That I didn't care about anyone except myshelf. That I didn't care about relationshipsh, or about feelingsh, or about what'sh happening right in front of me unlessh I thought it'd make a good picture, and then all I cared about was-sh getting the picture."

"And?" says Mr. Rent.

Scab shrugs. "Then she walked out."

"What have you been doing since then?"

Scab shrugs again. "Walking."

"And cutting yourself. What did you do it with?"

"A knife."

Mr. Rent looks at Scab and shakes his head. "You look goddamn awful." He takes Scab's glass and pours him another brandy. "Do your parents know where you are?"

"No."

"You have to call them."

"No."

"Then I'll call them. You can stay here tonight, but we have to let them know where you are. They'll be worrying."

"Don't tell them about . . . You know. Tell them we're working — a fire, or shomething."

After making the call, and speaking soothingly to Mrs. Faye, Mr. Rent pours another drink for himself and a third brandy for Scab, and says, "Your mother's not pleased — with you or with me."

"Thanksh. Sh-sorry."

"What did your folks say when the girl ran out?"

"Asked me what was going on, and when I told them what had happened, Ma said she didn't blame her and was ashamed of me — of what I'd become — and Pa said he was glad I was going away, and the sooner I went, the better. Not to bother coming back."

Mr. Rent settles himself beside Scab. After a few minutes, he says quietly, "She had to find out sooner or later."

"I know."

"I hate to say it — but I did warn you."

"I know."

"You can't afford to get involved with anyone in this business."

Scab thinks of Mr. Rent's photo of the beautiful, mysterious Vietnamese girl.

"I'm not involved."

Mr. Rent looks at Scab. "Right."

The music stops. While Mr. Rent puts another CD on, Scab pulls a photo of Philomena from his pocket. It's a close-up of her face as she bends over the old woman in the candlelit shed in the alley.

Mr. Rent sees him looking at the picture. He stands behind Scab and puts his hand on his shoulder. "It's tough, losing a friend."

"I guessh."

"A friend-not-quite-just-a-friend."

"What d'you mean?"

"You know what I mean."

He takes Scab's glass and his own. "One more, eh? You're not going any further tonight, are you?" He fills them, hands one to Scab, and holds up his own in a toast.

"Here's to many more friends-not-quite-just-friends. But meanwhile — think what you've achieved. You're off to college to study something you love. You've won a major award that'll set you up for a career in photojournalism. And you're already a success with your camera. What else matters?"

They settle back in their chairs, drinks in hand, listening to the music.

After a while a silence falls across the room. Scab looks over at Mr. Rent. He's passed out.

Scab turns, and leans back in his chair, looking into the darkness of the harbour.

HARBOURSIDE HIGH SCHOOL - SAINT JOHN
Final Report Card

Student: Julian Faye

Grade: 12

Home Room: Mr. Kinney

SEMESTER	YEAR TO DATE
Days absent: 12	Days absent: 27
Times late: 25	Times late: 53

COMMENTS KEY

1 - Pleasure to have in class.
2 - Good class participation.
3 - Keep up the good work!
4 - Puts forth effort.
5 - Conscientious student.
6 - Neat and accurate work.
7 - Contributes intelligently.
8 - Tries hard.
9 - Shows little interest.

SUBJECT	PERCENT	COMMENT
English Language Arts	89%	9
Julian has the ability to do so much more, if he cared to put his mind to it.		
French Language	75%	9
Mathematics	63%	9
Science & Technology	60%	9

SUBJECT	PERCENT	COMMENT
Social Studies	84%	9
Health & Phys. Ed.	45%	9
The Arts	95%	9

A strange student, whose work is good but who seems not to care.

Principal's Message:

You've turned out a fine young man, Julian. We're proud of what you've made of yourself.

Mr. B.J. Wood
_____

Mr. B.J. Wood
B.A. B.Ed. M.Ed.

Read more great teen fiction from SideStreets.

Ask for them at your local library, bookstore, or order them online at www.lorimer.ca.

Out
by Sandra Diersch

No one in Alex's world is who they seem to be. Alex struggles with his faith when he witnesses a church member cheating on his wife and learns that his brother is gay. When his brother is brutally attacked, Alex is forced to decide where his loyalties lay and what he really believes in.
ISBN:978-1-55277-421-2 (paperback)

New Blood
by Peter McPhee

After a gang of thugs beat him up, Callum's parents decide to move. But the problems don't end for Callum in their new town. Callum's deep inner scars make school a continuous battleground.
ISBN:978-1-55028-996-1 (paperback)

Wasted
by Brent R. Sherrard

Jacob likes to party, but, unlike his alcoholic father, he knows that he can easily overcome his drug and alcohol abuse. When a terrible tragedy takes Jacob to the breaking point, he discovers just how powerful dependency can be.
ISBN:978-1-55277-419-9 (paperback)